Béla Bartók's *1907 Violin Concerto*: Genesis and Fate

Sources and Studies in Music History from Antiquity to the Present

Edited by Elliott Antokoletz and Michael von Albrecht

Volume 50

PETER LANG

Alicja Usarek-Topper

Béla Bartók's *1907 Violin Concerto*: Genesis and Fate

PETER LANG

B Bibliographic Information published by the Deutsche Nationalbibliothek
The Deutsche Nationalbibliothek lists this publication in the Deutsche Nationalbibliografie; detailed bibliographic data is available in the internet at http://dnb.d-nb.de.

Library of Congress Cataloging-in-Publication Data
A CIP catalog record for this book has been applied for at the Library of Congress.

Cover image: Sketch/Drawing by Austin Topper (author's son)

ISSN 0175-6257
ISBN 978-3-0343-3574-4 (Print)
E-ISBN 978-3-0343-4039-7 (E-Book)
E-ISBN 978-3-0343-4040-3 (E-Pub)
E-ISBN 978-3-0343-4041-0 (Mobi)
DOI 10.3726/b16798

© Peter Lang GmbH
Internationaler Verlag der Wissenschaften
Berlin 2021
All rights reserved.
PL Academic Research is an Imprint of Peter Lang GmbH.

Peter Lang – Berlin · Bern · Bruxelles · New York · Oxford · Warszawa · Wien

This publication has been peer reviewed.

www.peterlang.com

In Memory of Elliott Antokoletz

Preface: The Author's Reflection

Inspired by his music and motivated by his letters from the past, I devoted three years at the University of Texas at Austin to Béla Bartók's remarkable *1907 Violin Concerto* in order to bring to light what required a half-century to bring to sound. In my research I drew upon primary sources, including materials in the Paul Sacher Stiftung in Basel, Switzerland, as well as upon the analytical evidence the *Concerto* score reveals. What follows is the story behind this seminal but long-lost work that explains what happened and what for so long did not happen. I reflected on what the young composer and musicologist wrote to his beloved Stefi Geyer in the early spring of 1907: "While working on it I have always your art of playing in mind. Otherwise, I would not compose it. I am doing it only for you."[1] Then I reviewed some words accompanying a book I had received in 2004 from the late Elliott Antokoletz with a different dedication and an invitation to convert my dissertation into a book. Motivated and enthused by his expression of support to publish with the house for which he served as music editor, I once again opened my dissertation in standard University of Texas orange to learn anew what I had written. While reading the opening chapter and remembering what followed, I recognized that in fact a new assignment had been given to me–to write a book that would tell the whole story.

I wish Elliott could have seen the project finalized and hold this work in his hands. But I can still thank him, brilliant and genuine Bartók scholar, my friend, *Doktorvater*, and mentor, for his work and friendship, and at the end, mostly for the long distance phone calls that penetrated and touched life and music before he fell silent. After December 20, 2017, the personal words etched in his numerous books became my solitary lifeline to him and the worlds he had opened up for me, serving as both unending consolation and motivation. They likewise serve as cherished substitutes and loving souvenirs of the untold hours we spent together on our common passion during which I was the sole heir of his wisdom on music in general and Bartók in particular, and the lone recipient of his patience and encouragement. The long hours of conversations, energy of persuasion, and genuine care

---

1   Béla Bartók, *Briefe an Stefi Geyer, 1907–1908*, ed. Paul Sacher, German trans. by Lajos Nyikos (Basel: Privatdruck Ltd., 1979), no. 2, sec. 3. In my bibliographic citations the numbers do not refer to pages but rather to the ordering of the letters in Sacher's publication. The English translations of *Béla Bartók, Briefe an Stefi Geyer* are mine unless otherwise indicated. The facsimiles of the original Hungarian autographs of these letters can be viewed in the second half of this volume.

I will always gratefully remember. Antokoletz' Research Grant for *Bartók Scholarly Investigation*, which he passed on to me during my years at the University of Texas, enabled me to translate the German edition of Bartók's letters to Stefi Geyer into English and provided the additional support for my work. By then I was well schooled in his knowledge and scholarly enthusiasm which whetted my academic desires and awakened my sensibilities to Bartók's unique artistic language. "It takes both playing and understanding," he once said, to complete a study of a musical work. His faith in my project and his confidence in its completion were an encouragement I desired and needed. His request to "play the *Concerto* beautifully" before I appeared on stage assured me an abiding serenity at many performances.

What I found comforting during these past two years and more specifically what kept pushing me toward the neglected desk in our home kitchen was this persistent calling that Antokoletz desired this book and, as a result, so did I. The last of our many inspired Bartók conversations, which took place at his home in November 2017 just before his last Thanksgiving, was the one that brightened the room of my future. I would say to him that I cannot work as fast, talk as fast, sleep as little, rise at the "grey hour," and be so systematic as he. I have an artistic temperament, a revolutionary soul, and two plus two often does not equal four, and besides, my son, my young cello virtuoso at home, is a magnet in my life in more ways than two. He calmly replied that "these are good reasons and I always knew them, and I accept them today, but not tomorrow. . .the time is running out" –I did not know that I would have to accept these as his last words of a lasting today. When I glanced back at the receding house at Horse Shoe Drive, the light was still burning. And so I shall not repeat a mistake another has made and keep my orange dissertation locked up in some academic drawer. This story must be told in order to understand Béla Bartók more deeply by encountering a work that lies at the basis of his musical revolution and was co-authored in more ways than one by the woman in his life.

****

Just as the performance of a concerto requires a score, and a score needs a title to provide invitation and entry, so here too a brief word is apropos before the musical message begins. A genre can be reasonably defined after giving due allowance to such audacities as trespassing over borders, birthing new forms, and "cross-fertilization."[2] When we choose to listen to, say, a concerto, we are choosing a specific art form. The composer can lead us to the edges, but we must at least start out on settled estate. We know what we have chosen, and we have chosen to have our expectations met. And now today, on this special occasion, we decide

---

2   Term used by Nicholas Marston, *Schumann: Fantasie,* Op. 17 (Cambridge University Press, 1992), 30.

to listen to a violin concerto. We have chosen even more precisely by selecting this composer because we want his music. And we indulge our demands one last time by looking for a performer–the one we trust or the one we have heard can be trusted–and he is in town. So now the stage is complete: title, score, composer, desire sandwiched in the middle, conductor, setting, orchestra–a grand assembly where all parties come together to form an alliance of artistry.

So we now follow our desire and make our way to the concert hall for a live performance because music is principally alive. We have found a good seat (we can see the violinist), and before the music begins we immerse ourselves in the program notes and message about the *Concerto*. Then we learn that it was dedicated to her, his first love. She was a young virtuoso and he was a young composer. The saddest sentence of all informs us that she never performed her concerto and he never heard his dedication. We feel a disquieting premonition of what we will hear, how we will receive it, and whether we will truly understand it. I would therefore ask the reader to bear in mind that it was he, the composer, who transformed his desire into an intention, and his intention into a musical artifact and deed as we find in the *Violin Concerto*. We shall hear the music as a fragment of his life. From there one is led to other fragments–a trove of personal letters he addressed to her. And from them one is beckoned to a larger whole of which the music and the letters are parts.

This book is one musician's reflection on and reliving of a relatively unknown moment in musical history. Since the *Concerto* is a lyrical and elegiac work, we require a calmer medium, a poem, to make a point more subtly. Yet not all of us are poets. T. S. Eliot is:

> Time present and time past
> Are both perhaps present in time future
> And time future contained in time past.
> If all time is eternally present
> All time is unredeemable.
> What might have been is an abstraction
> Remaining a perpetual possibility
> Only in a world of speculation.. . .
> Footfalls echo in the memory
> Down the passage which we did not take
> Towards the door we never opened
> Into the rose-garden.[3]

In accord with standard genres and musical forms, Bartók's *1907 Violin Concerto* was grouped with his *Ideal* and *Grotesque* and may be called the "1907 Silent

---

3   Opening verses of "Burnt Norton," *The Four Quartets*.

Concerto" until it was rediscovered. But while waiting decades to spring back to life in the public domain, they left their mark on other early works of the young composer and helped shape the musical direction he would eventually choose.

1907 Violin Concerto's Dedicatee

Acknowledgments

So much gratitude to so many people in both my life and the life of my book must be expressed here. More people than this brief space can afford mention have helped shape me and supported my work over the years. Their energy in loving and example in living I will retain in remembrance of their generosity and my debt to their legacy.

My love and gratitude first to my husband Matson Topper, who over the past 19 years has accompanied me on my American journey and offered his love and comfort when I needed it most. His faith in this project and envisioning its publication ahead of me were an encouragement when it was most needed. And I am grateful for his humor and his smile. A special thanks to him for presenting me with two matchless 1907 antique photographs of Stefi Geyer, which he mysteriously found among the treasures of a Swiss photograph collector. I thank him for his kindnesses in the early mornings and late evenings, and for the moral support in between during long, hot Texas days. I extend my affection and gratitude to my son Austin, "the young cello virtuoso and artist,"[4] who drew the striking image of Béla Bartók on my book cover with the same hand that has displayed a gentle touch on the instrument and in family life over the past 15 years.

To my friend and American editor Sharla Schimelpfenig I offer my gratitude for invaluable hours of counsel and suggestions. Each time Sharla welcomed me at the coffee shop–our work place–with unwavering warmth and openness. She was sensitive to the minor chords and nostalgic yarns of an enthusiastic story writer and passionate violinist.

A thank you from the depths of my heart to Walter and Hinke Schroen for providing hospitality in their splendid home in Munich–the noble city on the Isar. The venerable living room window in *Jugendstil* brought me the first light of the "grey hour" and the first rays of sunshine on July mornings spent in solitude.

I owe an old debt of gratitude to Benjamin Suchoff for his kindness in serving as my external advisor in the distant past and afterward as "fun friend" before he left this world and is now very much missed.

Piotr Wojtania requires a deep measure of gratitude for formatting my cover picture and all the images in my opening chapter with his sharp photographic eye. He, his wife, and their daughter are family to me when we celebrate our great Polish traditions together, cultivating our roots, and nourishing the cosmopolitan spirits.

---

4   As described by mutual friends Elliott Antokoletz and Peter Salaff.

Tim Shaffer, Austin Symphony trumpeter and old University mate, receives my gratitude for assistance on the musical inserts and *Violin Concerto* score excerpts.

I express my gratitude to Lawrence Donohoo, lasting friend and soulmate. I cannot begin to thank him enough for helping me clarify philosophic thoughts, especially those written in German, and for his untiring efforts to understand and follow my spirit in its "heartstrong" search within the music. Listening before I would begin to speak and knowing my motivations often left unsaid were more than comforting. And looking further into the past, I thank him for the continuous assistance, support, love, and inspiration shown to me across the years and often across two continents. His restless mind and worldly enthusiasm have sparked my aesthetic desires and awakened my sensibilities to moral truths and artistic language.

My last expression of gratitude is reserved for Michael von Albrecht. You have offered me a consoling serenity. I know that your heart grieves with mine and hears the same strange quietness after Elliott's departure. Thank you for our Friday evening phone conversations. And thank you for making this opus possible.

Contents

Prologue

Béla Bartók's oeuvre includes five concertos for solo instrument and orchestra: two for violin (1907–1908 and 1937–1938) and three for piano (1926, 1930–1931, and 1945).[5] The first and last of these five have personal dedications. Bartók's *1907 Violin Concerto*, which represents his first foray into that genre, was composed for his first love, the young Hungarian virtuoso violinist Stefi Geyer. The *Third Piano Concerto* (1945), which represents his late thought in the genre, was written for his second wife, Ditta Pásztory.

A posthumous work, the *1907 Violin Concerto* is of interest for three major reasons: it was the only one of his early masterworks that the composer withheld from publication, it was never performed during his lifetime, and it served as a quarry from which he frequently pilfered for his later works. Unlike Bartók's later works, the *Concerto* juxtaposes rather than fuses various sources, specifically German late-Romantic expressions, recent French impressionism, and indigenous folk styles of divergent Eastern European regions. After withdrawing the work from publication, Bartók revamped the first movement and converted it into the first of two symphonic poems entitled *Two Portraits*, op. 5 (1911). Thematic material from the *Concerto* also found its way into the *First String Quartet*, op. 7 (1908–1909); the *Fourteen Bagatelles*, op. 6 (1908); "A Portrait of a Girl," the first of *Seven Sketches*, op. 9b (1908–1910) that was dedicated to his first wife Márta Ziegler, *Second Elegy*, op. 8b (1909); and the opera *Bluebeard Castle* (1911).

The inspiration for the *1907 Concerto* was Bartók's image of and love for Stefi Geyer, and it was her rejection of his love that not only marked the end of their relationship, but also sealed the fate of the composition. She received it but chose not to perform it. The work's high degree of extra-musical significance is expressed primarily by the use of leitmotifs, some of which Bartók himself named and identified in his letters to Stefi from that time. A Tristan-like motif and its variants and transformations symbolize Stefi Geyer and function as two manifestations of her character: the first an image of Bartók's Stefi as ideal woman, and the other an image of her as self-assured virtuoso. [**Postcard 1**]

---

5   A *Viola Concerto*, begun in New York, remained unfinished at the time of the composer's death in 1945.

Steffi Geyer, Violinvirtuosin.

Postcard 1

— (Eingefandt.) Es wird mit fogenannten
Wunderkindern viel zweifelhafte Reklame ge=
trieben und die Kunst damit mißbraucht. Wir
machen uns diefes Vorwurfs nicht fchuldig,
wenn wir in der Wochenchronik die 16=jährige
Stefi Geyer, Violinvirtuofin aus Budapeft,
welche am künftigen Dienstag in der Tonhalle
Zürich konzertiert, den Lefern im Bilde vor=
führen; denn die jugendliche Geigerin aus dem
Ungarlande, die Tochter des dortigen Dr. Geyer,
wird von den hervorragendften Blättern Oefter=
reichs, Italiens und Frankreichs als ein Natur=
wunder und als ein Wunderkind bezeichnet. So
fchreibt die „Neue Freie Preffe": „Das wahrhaft
überzeugende Talent ift das Entzückende von
der vom Wiener Publikum mit begreiflichem
Ueberfchwang aufgenommenen Erfcheinung. Wer
eine Cantilène fo zu fingen, fo zu phrafieren
vermag, wie die kleine Geyer, der ift ein geborner
Mufiker. Man kann fich dem Eindrucke von etwas
Rätfelhaftem, Wunderbaren nicht entziehen."

**ZÜRCHER WOCHEN-CHRONIK 1906 NR 2
(13. JANUAR 1906)**

Postcard 1 (Back of the **Postcard 1**)[6]

The work's high degree of extra-musical significance is expressed primarily by
the use of leitmotifs, some of which Bartók himself named and identified in his
letters to Stefi from that time. A Tristan-like motif and its variants and transformations symbolize Stefi Geyer and function as two manifestations of her
character: the first an image of Bartók's Stefi as ideal woman, and the other an
image of her as self-assured virtuoso.

Three significant leitmotifs, each with the corresponding emotion of love,
grief, or desire, form the essence of the *Concerto's* compositional embodiment.
Echoing Tristan's pursuit of Isolde, Bartók expressed his feelings toward Stefi

---

6   A summary: Sixteen-year-old virtuoso violinist, Stefi Geyer from Budapest, has been
identified in Zurich as a prodigy child pleasing the audience with her genuine talent
and sincerely fantastic performance.

by sounding allusions to Wagner's apotheosis of unrequited love: the passionate form that is the highest love of all and the ardent despair that sharpens reality. Both passions–each truly heroic and tragic–elevate the desire for love fulfilled in the moment of death.[7] At the same time, Bartók was realistic in recognizing the struggle of a tender but anguished bond. As such, the music in the *Concerto* undoubtedly reflects Wagner's fervently idealized embodiment of humanity which Béla identifies with the hero Tristan. And as the drama of life and compassion continues in the music, both of its characters, Béla and Stefi, take on larger and more significant lives. Their "ideal" dawns and dusks seem to pass through the narrow tunnel of pain and discord that finally leads to a nostalgic and shadowy embrace.

Like a hanging note on an old calendar of events, the leitmotifs remind us of the evocative past of Béla and Stefi, sometimes to the point of reassurance, and inspire us to seek their significance in the concerto of their lives. This search is undertaken in the recognition that recovering the history partly depends on the music, and that the sounding leitmotifs immortally reflect what is now forever past. When we listen thoughtfully to the first unfolding of the *Concerto's* love motif, a chant of rejection emerges like a worried sensation in our emotional expectation. This, too, is a powerful feature of the leitmotif notion, which undeniably speaks a truth that transcends the actual experience of any two people.

Our characters, Béla-Tristan and Stefi, might find a very real place in our compassion and affection rather than be met with a curt dismissal or disapproval. This becomes easier when we see that Bartók is freeing himself from the bonds and conventionalities of archetypal Wagnerian human heroes–think of Tannhäuser, Lohengrin, and Siegfried. Even though they seem truly human, alive, individual, we must recognize their divine power. Lohengrin yearns for the woman who will believe in him and love him unconditionally for who he is, and whose love will endure despite everything. In contrast, Bartók's Tristan, like Shakespeare's passionate Romeo, finds the epitome of love not only in life but also in death. And yet the "Béla-Tristan hero" does not desire to die but to stand alone at the very summit of the ideal poetic world as the one supremely affected by the delight and misery of love and friendship and, in the end, their loss. In a letter to Liszt on Schopenhauer, Wagner admits that he has never experienced the true happiness of love in his life:

---

7   It involves the paradox that the lovers have found the path to their illusional happiness by means of an impossible relationship that uses an approach that distances them further from that relationship.

> I will erect one more monument to this most beautiful of all dreams, in which from beginning to end, this love shall fully satisfy itself: I have planned out, in my head, a *Tristan* and *Isolde*, the simplest but most full blooded musical conception, with the "black flag" that floats at the end, I will then cover myself up–to die.[8]

Stefi's *Concerto*, then, becomes an eternal elegy that does not die, for in music the fleeting passions of love endure forever.

In straining toward enduring meanings, Bartók's music becomes distinctly metaphysical, crafted by a composer driving to the roots of philosophic truths. But the foundation of musical thought and source of inspiration lie in the simple volition of pure life–in Tristan's will to live and enthusiasm to sacrifice. Inspired by Stefi, the *1907 Concerto* further reflects a romantic creativity that truthfully lies in Bartók's heartfelt soul and is expressed in his music. However, to transform unfulfilled longings into something attainable, Bartók also draws upon authentic folk sources that give voice to the humble truth of peasants. In this way the *Concerto* plays a crucial role in his development as a composer and individual being. It reflects a path that leads from the idealized, "romantic" world of Stefi to the real world of the peasant. But the path needs a long bridge over the wide river separating the ideal and the real, and that bridge is the earnest spirit of Tristan that spans these two jealous worlds. Biography and allusions to Tristan thus supply important keys for understanding the cryptic message in "Stefi's *Concerto*." This study will investigate all these issues that are both internal and external to the music of the *Concerto*, and thereby seek to come to an understanding of its musical poetry in relation to both the composer's music and words, passions and thoughts that are revealed in the larger whole of his letters to Stefi Geyer and the *Concerto* manuscript itself.

Now one may ask how poetic a nonverbal art may be. Perhaps it is just enough to speak about the romantic sphere that it reflects. The hidden message, whose theme is the inner self, exists both in the piece as a whole and in each moment of the composition. Thus one cannot help but perceive the *Concerto* from the position of a Romantic who is aware of Bartók's musical and aesthetic goals, and who acknowledges its significance as a work of programmatic music in all of its sophisticated and personal depictions of two characterizations of Stefi. These are an articulate and refined use of musical language and its tightly-woven design. Bartók's musical expression here shows a particular intention of thought and experience that implies universal values. Stefi's *Concerto* is then an important

---

8   William F. Apthorp, "Some of Wagner's Heroes and Heroines" (Scribner's Magazine, Vol. 5, 1889), 331–348.

witness to his life, one in which the young composer communicates his most profound being.

In light of the genre tradition, Bartók's *Concerto* evokes a number of related questions. Why does the work have only two movements? Why did Bartók transform the first movement into a sort of symphonic poem? Why was the work published only after Bartók's death? And, finally, why does the *Concerto's* basic thematic material reappear in many of his later works? One avenue to some answers lies in the following fragment of Bartók's diary from January 14, 1908:

> Once in a while, every few days, it feels as if my heart were beating the wrong way, as if it would send the blood on a side street. After such an unsuccessful heartbeat I always feel as if something just really tired me out, even though I was at complete bodily rest. Strange! For a long time, I have known this irregular heart beat but until now it was content with only one visit per year. But now, since my *Violin Concerto* or rather *Your Concerto* has been finished, it is my daily visitor. The muses ask us mortals to pay a high price for the inspiration. Much has happened in these days or perhaps nothing, depending on how you want to look at it.[9]

This depiction of heightened dramatic creativity is what Bartók could have but did not tell us in his *1921 Autobiography*. Undeniably, however, we experience it in his first solo work, the *1907 Violin Concerto*. Realizing this also leads us to understand why, under the circumstances of its genesis and rejection, he preferred for us not to hear a work that he felt revealed too deeply his personal and emotional secrets. Yet music must be performed in order to be heard and understood. Stefi could not hear Bartók's musical message, for there is no evidence that she ever performed it.[10]

---

9   Béla Bartók, *Briefe an Stefi Geyer, 1907–1908*, ed. Paul Sacher, German trans. by Lajos Nyikos (Basel: Privatdruck Ltd., 1979), 61. Nyikos explains that the quotation placed above originally belonged to Bartók's diary entries from an octave booklet that he had ripped out from it and then sent to Stefi Geyer together with Letter No. 25 on February 8, 1908. [65]

10 The autograph copy of the *Concerto* together with Bartók's letters to Stefi are in the possession of Paul Sacher and his Foundation. In 1958 the *Concerto* was performed under his baton at the Basle Bartók Festival.

1 1907

Photograph 1 (Budapest, April 7, "Sunday Finger" Magazine)[11]

Sunday Finger is the translated title of the magazine above, which "points the finger" to the artistic and musical life in Budapest. [**Photograph 1**] The April 7, 1907 issue details the current culture and embodied traditions of this glorious city. One may well wonder whether 1907 was an important year for Béla Bartók as well. While his *1907 Violin Concerto* is the subject of this book, a reading of his *1921 Autobiography*[12] or any of the earlier biographies written by the composer offers no indication of the *Concerto's* existence. Instead, one is led to believe that 1907 was of no special significance or turning point in the young composer's life, much less a starting point for the first of his master works.

As background to 1907, we need to examine the broader spectrum of Bartók's development. He began his career deeply rooted in the Germanic music tradition, having intensively studied the ultra-chromatic scores of Wagner and Liszt at the Royal Academy of Music in Budapest. During the first decade of the twentieth

---

11 A weekly magazine featuring Budapest current events, 269–288.

12 Béla Bartók, *Essays*. Selected and Edited by Benjamin Suchoff (University of Nebraska Press: Lincoln and London, 1992), 408–411.

century, Hungary was in the throes of a national movement that began with the Revolution of 1848. The search for cultural identity led to a reaction against the ultra-chromaticism of the Wagner-Strauss period. Having heard the rendition of a popular art song or urban folk song sung by a Hungarian peasant girl, Bartók was led to an awareness of a performance style quite different from the gypsy style of the cafes. This paved for him a way out of the German sphere of influence. In 1906, he began to collect the peasant music of the villages with Zoltán Kodály. From 1906 on Bartók became immersed in folk music investigations, which led him in 1907 to the discovery of the importance of the pentatonic scale in the Hungarian folk tunes. At the same time, his discovery of Debussy's music reinforced his awareness and use of the pentatonic scale. Also in 1907, Bartók joined the "piano staff" at the Academy of Music in Budapest (now the Liszt-Ferenc Academy of Music) at the age of 25. He crystallized the importance of this pedagogical employment in a few words:

> When an appointment to the chair of piano teaching at the Academy of Music in Budapest was offered to me in 1907 I considered this a happy event because it enabled me to settle in Hungary and to continue my studies in musical folklore. In 1907, at the instigation of Kodály, I became acquainted with Debussy's work, studied it through thoroughly and was greatly surprised to find in his work "pentatonic phrases" similar in character to those contained in our peasant music. I was sure these could be attributed to influences of folk music from Eastern Europe, very likely from Russia. Similar influences can be traced in Igor Stravinsky's work. It seems therefore that, in our age, modern music has developed along similar lines in countries geographically far away from each other. It has become rejuvenated under the influence of a kind of peasant music that has remained untouched by the musical creations of the last centuries.[13]

What we learn from this autobiographic excerpt, so typical of the kind of information that Bartók shares, is only a few basic facts, befitting more an academic vita than insight into the composer's creative process. What Bartók does not share with us are the revelations–personal and emotional crises–that inspired his creative genius. It is both shocking and disappointing that the entry on 1907 does not offer what we were hoping to find–the events of his life that led to the intense passion of the *1907 Violin Concerto*. Those who perform this work and are acquainted with the composer's personal correspondence know that it remained a critical year for him in both his personal and professional life. Armed with this additional source, the *Concerto* will reveal to them the joys and sorrows, successes and sufferings of Bartók's life. To confirm these suppositions, we must supplement the autobiographical evidence that he fortunately left behind with his personal correspondence and photographs of that time.

---

13 Béla Bartók, *Essays*, 408–411.

Szalatnay Benő fényképe.

GEYER STEFI HEGEDŰMŰVÉSZNŐ.

Photograph 2 [14]

What is clear above all is that the year 1907 is not an imaginary figment of a love story missing from Bartók's biographical statements. For in the 1907 magazine pictured at the beginning of this chapter, I discovered a beautiful photograph of Stefi Geyer, the violinist whom Bartók deeply loved. [**Photographs 2 and 3**]

---

14 Magazine "Sunday Finger" (Vasárnapi, Ujság), Budapest, April 7, 1907, 274.

Photograph 3 [15]

A few lines of the magazine are devoted to reporting that she was to be painted by a local artist and that her image would be displayed at the Franz Joseph University.[16] **[Photograph 4]** Today a number of other images of Stefi Geyer are extant. But her musical portrait *is* the *1907 Violin Concerto* that Béla Bartók personally dedicated to his beloved and that found in her its origin and purpose. This is the image of Stefi that was etched in the gallery of Béla's soul but would not be revealed for another fifty years.

From the summer of 1907 to the beginning of 1908, Bartók lived and worked continually in the "Tristan mood" of a passionately lofty love that illumined every moment of an inner world oscillating between a constant deluge of hope and of despair. This emotional whirlwind becomes the inspiration for both the *Violin Concerto* as well as a series of intimate and personal letters. The letters, in which the young composer also sets out his theses on his passion for the world, record the most important events in Bartók's life during this momentous period. And

---

15 **Photograph 3** shows the same image of Stefi Geyer within the text content on page 274 in the magazine itself. The text does not refer to the presented image.

16 On November 11, 1872 the Hungarian Royal University of Kolozsvár effectively opened its doors with four academic disciplines: Legal and Political Studies, Medicine, Philosophy and Science. In January 4, 1881 it was reconstituted as the Royal Hungarian Franz Joseph University. It remained an important center of science and education in the Austro-Hungarian monarchy.

Photograph 4 [17]

yet we discover that Bartók concealed this emotional background of primary significance when his romantic state of mind was obsessed with Stefi's motifs. While he tells her that "I live with you, in you, as if in a narcotic dream,"[18] he is unwilling to share this passion with the world. This narcotic dream, however, becomes the "idée fixe" for his entire work. According to Bartók, one requires such opium to brace the nerves, even if it can be toxic or ravaging in its effects.

The possibility of an underlying narrative concept in this first autobiographic solo work should not be dismissed simply because Bartók did not attach an explicit program. For his romantic relationship has been well documented by his letters to Stefi and perhaps even more dramatically by the music he composed at that time. We can therefore argue that this work lays bare the composer's feelings quite brilliantly and in a manner that only music can achieve. An idea mercilessly plagued Béla's mind and was unshakable: he was a total failure in both the domains of music and friendship. But one fine day, after receiving a particular

---

17 The Franz Joseph University with a view of Kolozsvár around 1900 (1907 Magazine "Vasárnapi, Ujság").

18 Béla Bartók, *Briefe an Stefi Geyer* (September 20, 1907), no. 11, sec. 1.

letter of Stefi, most if not all of the negative thoughts instantly disappeared.[19] A new hope awakened in his soul that flowers can still bloom–and even more beautifully can bloom on the field of conflict. Perhaps this is right, he admits, but who can know for certain?[20] For he observes that between them an eerie stillness has begun to appear–twists and turns, revisions without end. It looks as if they no longer have the courage to call things for what they are.

> I could really get scared, for I feel very insecure towards you; you, on the contrary, do not have to be afraid. You can be that way because you know everything about me. With a full and complete security, I write not only letters, but also notes. And what these ecstatic assumptions express is printed in this most clear and purest language. If you are a musician, you will be aware of it.[21]

In Bartók's writings about music, we encounter a passionate man who uses the melodic language of sounding tones to express his feelings. "I cannot imagine that an artwork could be anything but the manifestation of the infinite enthusiasm, despair, sorrow, vengeful anger, distorting and sarcastic irony of its creator."[22] This statement represents an integral perspective to Bartók's music and art. Thus in 1907, because of his love for Stefi Geyer, he desired to find the musical idiom that would express his romantic emotions, turning again to the highly expressive idiom of German music.

And so we assume from Bartók's statement about the autobiographical nature of his music that something significant was occurring in his life. It was a time when he had already established his methodology in the field of folk music research. It is also striking that he interrupted his folk music explorations in 1907 for this love relationship and became romantically involved with the young virtuoso violinist. Even though it was a time when he was searching for a way out from under the powerful influences of German Late Romantic music, it was this romantic musical source that was to serve his expressive emotional purposes.

---

19 Béla Bartók, *Briefe* (December 8, 1907), no. 20, sec. 1.

20 Ibid.

21 Ibid.

22 Judit Frigyesi, *Béla Bartók and Turn-of-the-Century Budapest* (Berkeley and Los Angeles: University of California Press, 1998), 11. This work is a beautiful reinterpretation of Bartók's aesthetic achievement as integrally interwoven into its historical milieu in early twentieth-century Hungary. In the context of discussing the role of Hungarian culture in the development of European modern intellectual and artistic currents, Frigyesi shows Bartók's connection with the inner circles of Hungarian intellectuals and explores the relation of his aesthetics to the poetry of such figures, among others, as Endre Ady or Béla Balázs.

Judit Frigyesi fills us in further: "Within the Hungarian romantic tradition, a poetry of intimacy that aimed at capturing moments of personal life. . .implied a style similar to folk poetry."[23] In addition to his folk-music research inspirations and his study of the French impressionist idiom of Debussy, Bartók's personal circumstances stood out in sharp contrast to all of the other musical factors which impacted his music before World War I. In distinction to the rest of his music that was typical of a compositional approach throughout his career, this musical period of several years was decidedly programmatic in nature, not only because of extra-musical associations with his compositions, but because they are all based on the same inspiration: his love for the beautiful Stefi Geyer.

The year 1907 thus establishes the powerful relationship between a young composer and a young virtuoso violinist that results in a musical manifesto of passions and unrequited love. Bartók's letters detail this relationship in the shattering words written in one of his letters in September of that year. He declared that after reading Stefi's letter he sat down at his piano with the tragic conviction that his comfort in life henceforth would be in music alone. And yet her leitmotiv (Bartók gives a musical outline of a minor seventh chord on the page of his letter: C#-E-G#-B#) haunted him and continued to dominate his heart. He goes on: "One letter from you, a line, even a word–and I am in a transport of joy, the next brings me almost to tears, it hurts so."[24] It stirs one's compassion to read such lines and seek an explanation.

The years 1907–1911 mark the appearance of Bartók's first masterworks.[25] It is striking that the very first of these is the violin concerto composed for Stefi Geyer as its dedicatee. The *Concerto* may in fact be considered a landmark in Bartók's compositional development on multiple levels. First, after two years of intensive immersion in folk music investigation, he found the ideal medium for his expression for his newfound love in the Wagnerian musical idiom. Second, it was a pioneering work in his progression toward the fusion of German romanticism, folk melodies, and Debussy's modality and pentatonicism. Third, it impelled him to work at the frontier between Western European art music and Eastern European folk music. Fourth, it animated the composer's struggle with

---

23   Ibid., 173.

24   *Béla Bartók Letters*, ed. János Demény (New York: St. Martin's Press, 1971), trans. Peter Balabán and István Farkas; trans. revised by Elisabeth West and Colin Mason (London: Farber & Farber; Budapest: Corvina Press, 1971), 86–87 (original letter in Hungarian).

25   We know that the *Violin Concerto* was neither "out there" nor on the list of master works. No one in public had known about its existence except Stefi Geyer, its dedicatee.

alternating moments of joy and rejection that will appear again in a later series of works of those years, as in his accommodating the "extreme opposite" to the initial *Ideal* character of the *Concerto* and depicting the decline of the woman in Bartók's opera *Bluebeard Castle*.

Finally and most importantly, all of Bartók's works from 1907 to 1911 belong to a unified conception based on Stefi's leitmotiv, which unfolds as early as the very first four notes of the *Concerto* (major-seventh chord outline: D-F#-A-C#). The chronological process of Bartók's first masterworks is underlined by a systematic transformation of Stefi's motif from the bright major third/major seventh to its brooding minor intervallic variants. This process reflects the movement from life-giving joy to despairing morbidity that delineates both a celebration of Stefi and a mourning for the loss of that relationship. Bartók himself refers to the latter as his funeral dirge,[26] which appears in the fugal opening of the *First String Quartet* as a statement on his painful grieving. And the funeral form represents Stefi's rejection of Béla and his own eternal loneliness in "endless night," a metaphor supporting his symbolic death.[27]

In February 1908 the personal relationship between Béla Bartók and Stefi Geyer came to an end.

> So, I have to take my leave-farewell forever now, because this is the last time that I am writing! The last time! So, on that Saturday then I played with you for the last time, and on Monday evening I spoke my last words to you at a barrier in the underground subway. For the last time I listened to you, for the last time I saw you. . ..
>
> The score of the *Violin Concerto* was finished on February 5th exactly the same day you signed my death sentence. I locked you up in a drawer. I don't know if I should annihilate you, or just leave you locked up there, and only perhaps someday after my death somebody will perhaps find you there. Then the whole paper stack will scatter in the wind: my love declaration, *your Concerto*, my best work–in the trash. I cannot talk about it, I cannot show it to anybody; this confession with its sad result does not matter to the whole world anyway.[28]

---

26 Denijs Dille, "Angaben zum Violinkonzert 1907, den Deux Portraits, dem Quartett op. 7 und den Zwei Rumänischen Tänzen" in *Documenta Bartókiana*, vol. 2 (Mainz: Schott, 1965), 92. See also János Kárpáti, *Bartók's String Quartets*, trans. Fred Macnicol (Budapest: Corvina Press, 1975; original Hungarian edition, Budapest: Zeneműkiadó, 1967), 173.

27 Dorothy Lamb Crawford, "Love and Anguish," *Bartók Perspectives*, eds. Elliott Antokoletz, Victoria Fisher, and Benjamin Suchoff (New York and Oxford: Oxford University Press, 2000), 132.

28 Béla Bartók, *Briefe*, no. 25, secs. 1 and 5. The score contains two different dates. The official information on the beginning and completion of the work is: Jászberény,

A year later in February of 1909, the people of Budapest could read Bartók's first essay on folk music and learn that

> [t]rue art manifests itself through the impressions taken from the outer world–under the influence of *experience*. If someone paints a landscape in order just to paint a landscape, if someone composes a symphony just to compose a symphony, then he is merely an artisan, in the best of cases. I can conceive of a work of art solely as a medium in which unlimited enthusiasm, despair, sorrow, angry revenge, burning scorn, and sarcasm of its creator finds expression. I used not to believe that until I found out myself that the works of an individual imparted more precisely than his biography the most portentous events and the defining passions of his life. . . . One could call the art music of the present–in contrast to the idealization of earlier periods–genuinely realistic. It seeks to give expression to all human emotions, randomly and honestly.[29]

It is hard not to conclude that Bartók was here referring to the *1907 Violin Concerto*. If this is correct, then the statement above serves as an honest and heartfelt reflection of his later emotional assessment regarding Stefi.

The guiding leitmotif, which provides the identity of the first movement and generates its architecture throughout, also serves as a reminiscence of the "ideal-motif" in several other compositions. He thereby laid the foundation for future masterworks to come, thus allowing for a dramatic-poetic unity in Bartók's life between 1907 and 1911. Stefi's leitmotif is a link to his unfolding experience–a whole stream of memories and reactions to them released from the composer's mind.[30] The quality of reminiscence is, of course, supported by the programmatic identification of Stefi's leitmotif as the "beloved" and underlies the *Concerto's* more global programmatic connection to the other works of that period. For the *1907 Violin Concerto* is the archetypal source of all of its offshoots because it is the faithful result and pure manifestation of Bartók's original feelings toward Stefi Geyer, the *Concerto's* dedicatee and inspiration. And she who recoiled from him since she could not return his love consequently serves as co-author of its darker variations. A threefold drama ensues for those who love to listen to the music, enjoy playing it, and read the private correspondence–the interpretative notes, as it were–and thereby access a world which Stefi and Béla in turn shared and shattered.

July 1st of 1907 and Budapest, February 5th of 1908. It is confirmed that 11 days later, on February 16th–the date marked by the composer on the first page of the score–Bartók sent the score to Stefi.

29 Leon Botstein, *Documentana Bartókiana*, Vol. 4. ed. Denijs Dille (Mainz: Schott, 1965), 78–79.

30 "This work repeatedly aroused him [Bartók] to many further compositions in which he executed stylistic experiments." Nyikos, Introduction to *Briefe*, 10.

2 Béla and Stefi: Auspicious Beginnings

The story of Béla and Stefi begins with their discovery and sounding out of each other in Jászberény. In order to understand the nature and importance of the Bartók-Geyer relationship with regard to its bearing on the *Concerto's* creation and its subsequent fate, we start with a love story about the young composer and the young virtuoso violinist as it is revealed in twenty letters, six postcards, notes written during Bartók's travels to collect folk tunes, a written diary, and of course the manuscript of the *Concerto* itself.[31] We will understand Bartók as an artist better if we recognize the roots of the young composer's work in the Romantic idiom as best suited for his need for romantic self-expression, and entertain the proposition that he created this work as an outpouring of unrequited love.

Béla's correspondence with Stefi supplies the key for our understanding of their relationship. These twenty letters detail his vacillation between happiness and sorrow in his references to Stefi as he painstakingly reworks the *Concerto*. They are a living testimony to the image of a putatively self-assured, but truly sensitive and easily hurt young man. This true story begins in Budapest early in 1907 after the twenty-six-year-old Béla Bartók assumed a post as professor of piano at the Budapest Academy of Music.[32] [**Photograph 5**]

Studying at the same Academy was the nineteen-year-old Hungarian Stefi Geyer. Born in Budapest itself, she was a talented and beautiful violinist studying under Jenö Hubay, a prominent and well-known violinist and pedagogue there. Bartók had met Stefi Geyer for the first time in 1903, four years earlier, when she was 15 and he was 22 years old. Both had been extraordinary students at the Royal Academy of Music in Budapest. We know that Stefi had been recognized internationally as a remarkable and highly gifted virtuoso violinist as early as 1903. A year later, as we noted, her concertizing trip to London assured her prestigious standing in the musical world of Europe. [**Photograph 6**]

---

31 A Bartók/Geyer Letter Chronology 1907–1908, based primarily on their correspondence, is placed in an appendix. Bartók was a very passionate but perhaps not very reliable correspondent who generally wrote letters only out of need or duty.

32 This was originally known as the Royal Academy of Music. In the same year, the Academy moved to a new building on Liszt Ferenc Street. In comparison with similar music academies in Europe, the acoustics of this concert hall with organ was described by Stravinsky as one of the world's best. The grand interior decor in an art nouveau style includes stained glass and short columns in gold and turquoise.

Photograph 5

Magyar művészek Londonban. Az angol fővárosban julius 6-ikán érdekes hangversenyt tartottak a királyunk védősége alatt álló *Ferencz József-intézet* javára. Előkelő bizottság rendezte, melynek élén a *Connaughti* herczeg, a *Walesi* herczeg és *Mensdorf-Powilly* gróf osztrák-magyar nagykövet állottak. A Londonban időző művészek legjelesebbjei működtek közre. Nagy hatással játszott hegedűn *Geyer Stefi* kisasszony, a fiatal hegedűművésznő, ki Hubay Jenőnek Carmen-átiratát eljátszván, a tapsok után még egy magyar ábrándot adott elő, ismét nagy lelkesedés közt. A hangverseny több mint 17,000 koronát juttatott az intézetnek. Nemsokára egy magyar festő gyűjteményes kiállítása is gyarapitni fogja a londoniak ismeretét a magyar művészekről. A londoni Continental Gallery igazgatója felkérte *Margitay Tihamért*, hogy Londonban műveiből kiállitást rendezzen. Margitay október hóban rendezi a kiállitást, s azon bemutatja «Rabiga» czímű nagyarányu festményét, a mely nálunk a Nemzeti Szalonban rendezett kiállitásról ismeretes.

Photograph 6 [33]

---

33   Magazine "Sunday Finger" (Vasárnapi, Ujság), Budapest, 1904, 501. This is a short "violin virtuoso write-up" announcing Stefi Geyer's concert trip to London in support of József Ferenc University.

In the early spring of 1907, the young piano faculty member Bartók, shortly after assuming his position, initiated a relationship with Stefi by making music with her. A little undated note card may be assigned to this period in which Béla announces his arrival in Jászberény, a little town southeast of Budapest, where Stefi and her brother enjoyed spending their summers:

> Dear gracious Madam,
> With your permission, I will come to see you at noon on Friday with a pile of scores. I will bring along some Strauss Lieder and other music. Would it be possible for you to get the Second Reger Sonata by then? See you soon and many regards.
>
> Your faithful
>
> Béla Bartók[34]

The note implies that the pair had discussed their musical repertoire prior to this planned visit and that both were excited about playing Max Reger's *Violin Sonatas* together.[35] In Bartók's subsequent letters to Stefi from the end of July through August, he often would ask her if they can "regern" together again, which in that context means playing Reger's music on and off throughout the summer of 1907.[36]

We can learn much about the young Béla from his correspondence with Stefi. In his letters of July and August, Bartók speaks often of his research in the field of folk songs and counterparts to it that he finds in his interpretations of compositions from the classical repertoire. But we learn something of greater importance from another undated letter written to Stefi from Rákospalota probably in the beginning of July. Bartók makes it clear that in several important matters he and Stefi have opposing convictions. As an example, he mentions their conflicting views about marriage and the traditional morality it implies. To Bartók's way of thinking, a man must remain free, even in marriage. This freedom is what he considers to be the true core of the marital bond in contrast to the romantic and sentimental ideal of eternal fidelity propagated by

---

34 Béla Bartók, *Briefe an Stefi Geyer*, no. 1. The original in the form of a blue color note card is lost. But it gives evidence of Bartók's move from Pressburg (Bratislava) to Rákospalota, a district of Budapest, likely in the early months of 1907.

35 According to Nyikos' notes, the first date that can be determined, July 1, 1907, is the day of Bartók's visit to Stefi Geyer in Jászberény.

36 Bartók may also be making a play on words here with the German adjective *rege* (lively, animated, buoyant). He visited with the German composer Max Reger in Leipzig during the summer of 1907.

organized religion and the popular middle-class romantic novels (*Gartenlaube*) of the time.[37]

> I stand with my principles quite in isolation, and I find nobody who could approve of them. Yet you should believe me when I claim all of that neither for the sake of something very odd and peculiar, nor because I believe that material comforts will increase, and in any case not out of cynicism; each of my words arises from solely honest and sacred conviction. I necessarily believe that only this form of marriage is moral; every other [form] is more or less immoral. For above all I do give a preference to the freedom of people and yet set limits to it. However, I have to admit that, after all that, when I was eighteen years old I did not think like that; rather, the "everlasting fidelity" of the "Gartenlaube"–the highest fiction of all–was then the only idealistic goal of life.[38]

Bartók points out that "nobody" out there approves of his nonreligious attitude in life and his modernistic philosophical orientation. To be isolated, however, was not uncommon for many artists influenced by Freudian psychoanalysis and its powerful effects. In fact, Bartók continues, loneliness is both the desired and essential potion to be poured into a meaningful life–the goal above all–a life transcending limits and extremes. And now such an existence is at hand for many in the European romantic tradition: inspired souls seeking the depth of the meaning of life and its fulfillment through art.

If we submerse ourselves in the fog of old Budapest and increase our effort to understand the thought process of many artists at the turn of the century–Endre Ady and Béla Balázs come first to mind–the prevailing views of the day begin to emerge. While previously sheltering the traditional cultural life of many artists, Budapest in the first decade of the twentieth century recentered its focus on modern art. In particular, the Hungarian intelligentsia shared a desire to discover a new paradigm to inseparably fuse the most polarized elements of culture and life. And the artists of the time joined this project by playing a significant part in seeking answers to the questions of life's meaning. This diversity within a larger unity becomes an essential concept for Bartók's work and life. Polarities and dialectic polemics occupy his thinking, observations, and attitudes. During this period, he searched for new ideals that would unequivocally establish his relationship with the outer world. Frigyesi observes: "By 1908 the cardinal points of Bartók's worldview and aesthetics had crystallized around an ideal that aimed at drawing all life's diverse and polarized aspects into an intensely unified vision."[39]

---

37 These novels expressed sentimental romanticism and unrealistic truisms for those who liked to see them covertly present in the sweet gardens of their lives.

38 Béla Bartók, *Briefe*, no. 2, sec. 1.

39 Frigyesi, 170.

Within and perhaps before that unity, the division of life into polarities with its enormous load of symbolic meaning and metaphor becomes a speeding vehicle that carries extreme emotions into the existential search for life's purpose. Ernő Lendvai, writing nineteen years after the composer's death, recognized that the development of divergences grounds Bartók's tonal language with a significant and specific poetic theme that unifies opposites within such conflicting settings.

> What differentiates Bartók's piece from Tristan's yearning for night, and from Wagner's and Nietzsche's belief in the redeeming power of the idea of nirvana, is precisely the balance between the conceptions of light and darkness, day and night, life and death. The pessimism of the piece (if it is pessimistic at all) lies not in the power of the night that swallows up everything but rather in the thought that the dialectic unity of dark and light is a necessity. . . . Bartók's world is a world of polarity: it is neither "dark" nor "light" but it is dark *and* light. Both are always together, in inseparable unity as if polarity were, for him, the only framework in which a conceptual and dramatic message could manifest itself.[40]

For Bartók, then, a conception of polarities and juxtaposition between idealistic Romantic poet and real loving peasant is the principle he often uses to explain himself better and convey to Stefi his personal thoughts and general ideas of life. "On Sunday I was still comparing your hand [Stefi's] with mine; on Tuesday, however, I held the sunburnt hand of a peasant-girl. On Sunday I spent the night in one of the most noble chamber-rooms, whereas on Tuesday I got my rest in a peasant house."[41] We wonder if Bartók's comparisons are intended to simply feel the gentle weight of another's hands in his own or to place one "hand" above the other–the elegant and noble above the real and provincial peasant. Or, maybe it is more of a temptation to follow the romantic sentiment to feel what is imperceptible. Frigyesi supports this last interpretation when she further notes that Bartók "did not trust language to express the most important things in life. Nor does it suggest a belief that language cannot express anything at all. . ... Only things of the greatest significance were inexpressible."[42] Instead, he used music as his primary communication for great thoughts and powerful feelings. The *1907 Concerto* magnificently manifests this dramatic concept of polarization within a musical language that narrates the story of opposite feelings.

In an early July letter from Rákospalota, Bartók also mentions that he is working on a new composition for violin–without doubt, the *Concerto*. But he

---

40 Lendvai, *Bartók dramaturgiája*, 66 in Frigyesi, 292.
41 Béla Bartók, *Briefe* (Rákospalota, July of 1907), no. 2, sec. 2.
42 Frigyesi, 8.

wonders whether Stefi will treat his new composition with the same kind of indifference that she gave his *Serenade*.[43] If this were to happen, he would find it very
painful "because while working on it I have always your style [art] of playing
in mind. Otherwise, I would not compose it. I am doing it only for you. By the
way, is it possible that I misunderstood you–already in Jászberény, I could not
figure out the riddle that you are for me. Has your ecstasy cooled off already?"[44]
In his next letter, dated July 14th, it is clear that Stefi did respond to his letter,
but either she did not understand Bartók's questions or did not answer them
honestly. She apparently thought that he had been "fishing for compliments" or
perhaps she may have wanted to get even with him regarding a similar situation that had transpired earlier when the roles were reversed. For in an earlier
undated July letter to Stefi, we learn that he attended one of her recitals in which
she performed Bach's *Chaconne*. It seems that he upset her afterwards by not
commenting on her playing, and so he needed to explain himself:

> It came to me belatedly that you may be wondering why I did not exchange any words
> with you regarding your recent Chaconne-Lecture-Recital. Frankly speaking, all those
> waxen "Salonlobsprüche" [flattering compliments] after your performance I found very
> unpleasant, but since I was unable to outdo them, I had no choice other than to remain
> silent. Anyway, after the performance of a great artist it is not proper to give any kind
> of praise; but only to show gratitude and say "thank you." All the rest, then, should be
> judged as being closer to disagreeable than satisfying.[45]

Because Stefi made no comments after this letter, then reacted with indifference
and silence after Bartók's performance of the *Serenade*, and finally expressed no
interest in sharing a few words, he feared the worst–another misunderstanding–
and therefore made an additional attempt to clarify his opinion and perception
of both situations.

As one might expect, there is also a casual side to this relationship: Bartók
asks about Stefi's brother and his examination results, and anxiously questions
when she will be returning to Budapest. After receiving her response, Béla
acknowledges that it has given him much joy to hear her voice in the "desolate
wasteland" near Csikrákos. He shares with Stefi the daily affairs of his field work
while traveling.

---

43 Bartók refers to *Serenade* here, but we have no listing in any of the existing published
     catalogues of this title.
44 Béla Bartók, *Briefe* (Rákospalota, Mariastrasse 15), no. 2, sec. 3.
45 Ibid., sec. 1.

I am here in the summer-fresh wasteland of Csikrákos. Such a drastically foreign manner of life I could not lead even in Africa. First, a gentleman invites me as his guest to the house; then, in the evening around 8:00 pm he gets so drunk that I could no longer stay. I left and found some help with a teacher, so together we looked for accommodations for me in the village until 11:00 pm, but without success. . . . As far as the food is concerned, the choices are monstrous. . . . Every day fresh lamb, raw. [Only] one who knows little about cooking may eat that way! Bacon, goat cheese, and dark bread are obtainable as well. . . . Tomorrow will be a whole week since I have had a warm meal.[46]

Despite this unappetizing fare, Bartók remained kind to his hosts by listening intently to their music to discover and record the distinctive sounds of the *Ballades*. It is for him both a joy and surprise that these melodies are still alive and pass through the lips of many who live there. "I hear the strange–at the same time unique–language that almost has vanished. . .the last breath and trades of a disappearing time is standing in front of me, the time that 40 to 50 years after me, no one will find."[47] Bartók adds a few musical quotations of the songs in *Parlando* style and questions their melodic origin as well as which scales or modes might be matched to their melodies. He enthusiastically notes that if there is more of such material, it would be tempting to identify and classify them as the "Alt-Székler" melodies. Clearly, much detailed sharing takes the friendship between Stefi and Béla to new heights and gives us solid grounds for seriously examining it. He confesses that it would make him happy to awaken her interest in the study of folk tunes, although his patronizing remarks make it clear that the more academic nature of his research is unsuitable for a performing musician.

Béla then chides Stefi for having not read any of the traditional classics, for instance, Tolstoy or Nietzsche, who often have commented in detail on this subject.[48] He asks why she prefers to rely on her own experience and the illusions of an idealistic and everlasting world and not take a stand against nineteenth-century theism.

Everyone has read the *Gartenlaube* literature by a certain age, if for no other reason than in the absence of better novels, or out of boredom. However, even we do not wish it, this reading has a small effect on us. You are missing the acquisition of knowledge; reading a few books can help. Among these, Nietzsche and Tolstoy are out of the question. That leaves us with the *Gartenlaube* kind such as Jókai, Romeo and Juliet–all praises of eternal fidelity."[49]

---

46 Béla Bartók, *Briefe* (Rákospalota, July of 1907), no. 3, sec. 1.
47 Ibid., sec. 2.
48 Ibid., sec. 6.
49 Ibid.

Bartók continues his tutoring and composes one more criticism of enduring feelings by proposing a hypothetical example:

> Two people live together in the shadow of the motto of enduring fidelity. Both are convinced of each other's importance. A third person is approaching. One of the two observes that it could lead to a crisis. He has only one opportunity to resist: he strongly and willfully refuses that third person. If he is successful and the third party disappears from the horizon, then everything is in order. But if the third person is not rejected by him and remains, then the coexistence of these two [of the original relationship] will be nothing more than cheating.[50]

He admits that enduring fidelity is feasible, but he values the truthful separation even more.

The Bartók-Geyer correspondence also discloses a less serious side to the relationship. For instance, he admits that he is both joking and earnest in his request: "Whether I can get an honest answer. It would make me so happy to engage in a deeper discussion, which is not as barren and therefore encouraging, as most evaluations tend to be. With your permission."[51] Bartók continues in serious but lighthearted tone:

> I will assign you a modest (humorous) homework concerning the Hungarian language (tongue speech):
> to spoil (in German): verwőhnen = elkényeztetni
> in both languages German and Hungarian, it requires
> 1 word
> I have been spoiled (in German): man hat mich verwőhnt = elkényeztette
> 4 words versus 1 word
> I am very happy that your brother passed the exam. My best wishes for a nice spa visit.
>
> Your faithful
>
> Béla Bartók[52]

The correspondence taken as a whole reveals that Béla is assuming that Stefi is interested in every detail of his life. In the subsequent letter from Csikkarcfalva dated on July 27th, he shares with Stefi a quite amusing episode of his research trips to Pest (the eastern part of Budapest) and Csikrákos.

> Dear gracious Madam,

---

50   Béla Bartók, *Briefe* (Rákospalota, Mariastrasse 15), no. 3, sec. 8.
51   Ibid., sec. 9.
52   Ibid., secs. 10–11.

1. What you call an interesting puzzle actually was a pretty unpleasant episode of my research excursion. One fine day early in the morning, my collector-colleague appears and with outrageous calmness reports the unfortunate event of his phonograph having been ruined. I immediately rushed to the next village to apprise myself personally of the situation. We found ourselves forced to conclude that henceforth he would have to collect without the machine. However, this was only the beginning. As soon as I returned home and began to work with my own phonograph, it became obvious that it, too, was suddenly ruined. Since I had already had trouble with the phonographs earlier on–the cylinders that were ordered did not arrive etc.–I packed my belongings, that is, my two ruined phonographs, and returned to Budapest on the first train. That way everything would quickly be all right again. The letter to you had already been written, so I took it with me to Budapest–which is in any case the more secure way. This, then, is the explanation for the strange date of the second letter. The first letter I wrote in Brassó; however, I could only mail it from Csíkrákos. But I could only give a return address of Rákospalota since I did not know when and where I would establish my base.

2. I arrived in Pest unbrushed, uncombed, dusty, filthy, in boots, with the appearance of a true burglar, and on the street had to hide myself so as not to be seen by any of my acquaintances. After taking care of my business, I went on to Rákospalota. There, to top it off, I got sick, and after an enforced rest period of one week, I traveled once again into the wasteland. These are my latest deeds.

3. In Csíkrákos I was immediately told that a letter from "Stefi Geyer" had arrived for me in Madaras. Because of my work, however, I could not escape from this damned Csíkrákos, where I only had troubles! Torments of Tantalus! To know that your letter was so close by, just about 20 kilometers, and not to be able to get it! Yet even the worst of today will have something of a highpoint–in the future. In Madaras, after I had received your letter, I had to talk with strangers for a long time–I could not open your letter. But finally, even that happened.

4. How can you only be so cruel to your own collector activity! How you ridicule and mock it! By the way, I am very impressed by the satirical tone you directed against yourself. There is something lofty about it when we can talk about our worn-out things in such a way: the "ego" becomes Lord and Judge of the "ego." On the other hand, I am sorry that you did not copy the two songs for me. I would terribly much like to know how your first attempt at collecting ended. How did it? Do you want to become my competitor in this field? *Bravo!* I will greet every new rival with great pleasure. We are too few as it is. And what a brilliant opportunity this opens for the Sunday paper to publish a sensational article.[53] "Stefi Geyer–folk song collector!" Picture 1: S. G. moves to Csíkrákos, squats on a hay wagon, and tightly embraces her phonograph. Picture 2: S. G. wades in boots through the filth of the main street of

---

53 We may assume that Bartók is referring to "Sunday Finger," in Hungarian "Vasárnapi, Ujság," a weekly magazine of current events in Budapest.

Csíkrákos, with her right hand holding a phonograph, with her left hand securing her skirt. Picture 3: Stefi is in the tavern surrounded by bold ruffians in fur boots. Picture 4: Stefi is thought to be a peddler.[54]

Bartók finally stops with his satire and in an appreciative line pays Stefi the compliment of writing about important and vital issues very beautifully and significantly. Nevertheless, he cannot resist a further criticism: "There, at the beginning of your statements is an 'on the contrary.' Here I say: unfortunately, to many of those 'on the contrary': Surely you don't need the heavier prize in the reading lesson? Why imagine them so fetchingly? Perhaps these were painted just in bad colors? On the Contrary! (Here I say, 'on the contrary')."[55]

Béla goes on to say that being caught between high society and bourgeois mediocrity is an absolutely unbearable situation. While Nietzsche associated mediocrity with the masses, which obviously includes the peasant class, Bartók assigns a different meaning to it. For the "lowest level" of society, that of the peasants, does not represent mediocrity but a world of escape from urban culture. It is the world and actions of the peasants with their pristine simplicity that he loved. In contrast, the intelligentsia, the upper level of society, manifest a highly developed way of thought and emotional distance. And yet his reflective observations concerning social class divisions manifest a distaste for mediocrity:

As far as tradition is concerned, only for the average person is it compatible with the Holy Scripture. But people like Stefi Geyer have been created precisely in order not to be placed under its yoke. For the lowest class–the people–the more they can cling to the tradition, the better. But people in the highest class must always free themselves from it more and more. There is no such thing as a middle way. Never has a maxim been more poorly advised than the one concerning the golden mean. It is not gold, but more worthless than everything else. For this reason the middle class, which stands between the upper class and the peasant class, is insufferable precisely in its narrowness. What we love in the peasants is their often pristinely strong and childish naïveté, which reveals itself in everything; in the upper class, intellectual strength imposes itself. But the stupidity of the mediocre–which include the greater part of "gentlemen"–is unbearable because they lack natural naïveté. I believe that everyone, women as well as men, must struggle against the chains of tradition, but only insofar as they possess the required strength to do so. The struggle is in fact nothing other than a striving for autonomy. We want to be dependent on no one, on nothing; we also want to be lord over ourselves. Perhaps this is the struggle against fate, which helps us precisely to this achievement of autonomy. When we harden ourselves in this struggle, we have made ourselves free from the instability of life within the limits of the possible. However, I can only imagine this as

---

54 Béla Bartók, *Briefe* (Csikkarcfalva, July 27, 1907), no. 4, secs. 1–4.
55 Ibid., sec. 5.

an ideal goal, which hardly anyone in fact will ever be able to arrive at. But it is an ideal precisely for this reason. (What exists can no longer be ideal.) We can only approach it to the utmost in proportion to our capabilities.[56]

It seems that Bartók is saying two things here: the Nietzschean way is superior in itself, but the simple way of the peasant is what we love and value. This is the contradiction, or at least the paradox, that he has to work through. It leads us to surmise that Nietzsche is not the only teacher for Bartók; so who is the other who is celebrating the peasant?

In the same letter of July 27th, Bartók asks Stefi if she has ever been concerned about or dissatisfied with the current state of affairs. For Bartók the critical thinker, absolutely nothing for him was in the right place. The world is inexplicable and therefore in many ways enigmatic. For example, he brings up the topic of his respected employment at the Royal Music Academy in Budapest.[57] After his appointment to the rank of professor, many in his circle said he could at last lead a quiet and completely satisfied life. He challenges that assertion, based as it is on the questionable value of striving for and then securing a stable position. This is in fact nothing other than a sluggish adiposity that chokes creativity and congeals in a corpulent overflow of greasy and dripping contentment.[58]

And yet, Bartók believes that only from an unimpaired and inclusive dissatisfaction can more significant deeds arise, and only from the result of discontent can one create a unique and independent work. There is yet more to his liberated thinking. Only one who can think autonomously and has learned the art of self-reliance is able to reject the existing order. In other words, he must act in defiance of the generally approved and favored. For an inability to act freely and exercise self-sufficiency rules out originality and excludes uniqueness. And such extreme discontentment must come naturally, unintentionally, unconsciously, for a genuine dissatisfaction with the way things are cannot be generated by an act of the will. This state leads to a stance of doubt and isolated superiority.

> [And] not to be misunderstood: from this dissatisfaction came the addiction to improvement, which was my greatest mistake.... At the price of bitter experiences, I have learned that this is a senseless, silly thing. . .. to challenge people, to burden them with something other than their own nature, is entirely impossible. How many agonies has this addiction caused me? With my next attempt, of course, I wanted a lot of things to have a very different outcome. It is clear that this desire came from a hidden selfishness: if I can shape someone according to my desires, dealing with them [as they are]

---

56 Ibid., no. 4, sec. 6.
57 Béla Bartók, *Essays*, 408–411.
58 Béla Bartók, *Briefe*, no. 4, sec. 9.

is far more enjoyable. How happy I was when I could forge my plans in advance! How pleased I was about the anticipated success. And then, what a crushing defeat on the first attempts. Some things in particular frightened me. I cursed my life, I wished my end....but I won. Now all this is over. I have secured my independence in this regard, eternally.[59]

Stefi is confronted with all of these weighty ideas. Is she among those who are to be challenged by something hostile to their nature?

Have they [your spiritual emotions] never spawned any doubts about what is truthful and really authentic? Or have you never known how to explore this? Have you never cared how another human (a poet or a writer) thinks about these things or did you recognize only as right and true what was presented to you as agreeable? Or have you never gagged or choked over such bagatelles? A lot of questions about the same thing, are they not? I would like so much to know your thinking, if only a few [thoughts]. Even after Jászberény, I was led by this desire to explore your thoughts and views.[60]

In fact, Bartók implies a complacent ignorance of these philosophical questions on Stefi's part. He relentlessly pursues his reproachful judgments and puts her on the spot by asking whether by any luck her thoughts might be latent? Quite a strong and egregious censure of a young girl who was trying to keep up with the well-read Bartók and his cognitively alien philosophy.

But at the end of this long letter, Bartók softens his language and shares some intimate, heartfelt feelings. He feels somewhat "strange" or maybe just alone and mystified, for everything seems more beautiful in Karcfalva than in the Csíkrákos region. He is not sure whether it is due to the more exquisite scenery or to something else. Béla admits that this feeling keeps him attentive and occupies his mind, and when that happens he is tempted to call it "his happiness." For some time now, the young sensitive composer has not felt that way. But Béla has no doubt that joy will soon disappear again–a matter of time–and that "grey" indifference will once again demand its place. "But this cannot be called pleasant even with the best intentions–the state of soul of the grey equivalence."[61]

According to Bartók's final assessment, the best antidote to all of these conflicting tendencies is forced cynicism. Nevertheless, he asks how she is doing and what she is doing the entire day. Has she taken some Reger music with her? "With due respect, what else one can find in such an ordinary elegant resort

---

59 Béla Bartók, *Briefe* (Csikkarcfalva, July 27, 1907), no. 4, secs. 9–10.
60 Ibid., sec.11.
61 Ibid., sec. 21.

town? Are you learning Italian?"[62] Bartók continues with a string of questions. But in the end he is sorry: "For so much writing, I really have to apologize. I appeal to your Christian values and feelings! But [again] it is not nice of you to ask for only two things to be forgiven; there were many more grandiose wrongdoings of yours."[63] And indeed, he points them out to her with a repetitive word of "etc. etc.," making no end to it. And yet for all that, Béla was less wordy than Stefi. Finalizing his eight-page letter, he apologizes for having written less than the twelve pages Stefi had written him. But to have written more would have been unbearable. With his adroit sarcasm and patronizing tone, Bartók's alternating conviction and uncertainty lead us to pose the question of where it all leads to.

The letter of August 20th returns to the subject of friendship. It includes a two-line song that Béla wrote to encourage Stefi to call him her friend: "I can see a friendship present only when the views on and opinions of the most important things are in harmony. ... Or, do I understand by friendship something different from what you do? Perhaps you have in mind a superficial comrade collegiality? In that case I would be very sorry."[64]

A dispute of selflessness versus selfishness follows in the same letter. Bartók explains that what holds for selflessness holds for egoism in terms of the cold and the warm. What he means by this is that the former is not the opposite of the latter, but only its diminished form. He argues further that if more warmth is felt, then we say it is warm, and if less, then it is cold.[65] An analogy is proposed:

> In Gyergyócsomafalva one measures the temperature of a spring: "Four degrees warm," it's called. Why doesn't the man rather say: "Four degrees cold"? The water isn't really warm; it's so cold that one can't stand it, as a farmer's wife would say. And she would be right. Here is a mistake in linguistic usage: warmth and coldness are set up as opposing terms.[66]

To apply the analogy: Bartók explains that selflessness, contrary to common opinion, is really nothing other than egoism at a lower temperature, and that sensual egoism is of a higher degree than spiritual egoism. For everything we do–that is, exercising our ego by acting–we do because it is more pleasant to

---

62 Ibid., sec. 24.
63 Ibid.
64 Béla Bartók, *Briefe* (Rákospalota, Mariastrasse 15, August 20, 1907), no. 7, secs. 2–3.
65 Ibid., sec. 7.
66 Ibid.

act than not to act. The mother suffering in place of her child finds this more pleasant than knowing that otherwise her child must suffer."[67]

Bartók explains his own connection to egoism further on in the letter and blames the drives within him as researcher and discoverer for causing him too many deprivations. Yet it is actually more pleasant for him to satisfy these drives at great cost than to abandon them. While the fame that he would receive from his discoveries does not tempt him, there is something quite gratifying in knowing that he treks down unknown paths and then returns home with such treasures like no one else. He admits that of course it would do him good if an earthly angel rewarded him for such selflessness of a "lower rank" since no human being could do so. But such a dream is vain. So we should wish to continue working without pause until we drop. For what else remains for us than suicide!

Having long since concluded to the futility of human existence and the meaninglessness of the entire earthly horizon, Bartók continues with this dark thought of human existence as the greatest tragedy of all with humanity wandering aimlessly. Since the belief in an earthly proprietorship and everlasting life makes no sense, we constantly deceive ourselves by finding a contrived interest in everything in order to avoid tormenting ourselves with the greatest human tragedy of all, namely, the insignificance of human existence.

> After having long since concluded that human existence is pointless and that the existence of the entire earthly universe has no meaning, what refuge would then still remain for me other than to clutch to strenuous labor like a sleeping pill? We deceive ourselves constantly, finding artificial interest in everything, so that we never have the occasion to torment ourselves with the greatest human tragedy: knowledge of the purposelessness of human existence.[68]

For the young composer, then, it is no longer an issue whether he falls sooner or later into the nirvana of the infinite. The strategy is to steer clear from the abyss through hard work. "Catastrophe would only then befall me when the joy of working were to cease and I would no longer be interested in anything."[69]

And right there in the midst of all these impassioned thoughts about the illegitimacy of humanity's high purpose, Bartók inserts a quotation of a six-measure piano score (the sixth bar having only a sign and the word "etc."). This musical phrase will become the first five measures of the opening of the second

---

67 Béla Bartók, *Briefe*, no. 7, secs. 7–8.
68 Ibid., sec. 9.
69 Ibid.

movement of the *Violin Concerto*. He then adds: "Was it not Stefi, the fearless and strong 14-year-old girl, whom I first met in Jászberény!![70] Hey! Hey! Hurry up, and correct your image, please, otherwise the whole piece will point to the following thing: 'G.[eyer] S.[tefi] when she is smoking a pipe.' "[71] [**Ex. 1**]

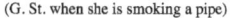

Example 1

"So, you equate a musician with a good 'pillar of society'? Hm! Strange! I would also like to draw your attention to the fact that I live not only on music, but also on many other things! Or have you noticed this before?"[72] In an earlier comment Bartók threatens that he might even use these measures for the work. And he did! The only difference between the measures quoted and the opening of the final version is that Stefi's "jagged" head motif is enharmonically spelled in sharps rather than flats.

Bartók brings up another important quotations written in French at the end of this letter, the first half of which he wrote in Csikrákos-Madéfalva. While traveling further and by the time he got to Pest, that first half of the letter got lost somewhere, possibly while changing trains. "Now I have replaced it, as best as possible. On the journey, I read the following lines of a wise man that shed light on that 'painful' question which we have already discussed in much

---

70 A typical allusion of Bartók that the 19-year-old Stefi hardly appreciated.

71 Here, at the beginning of the second movement for the first time and in its final form, the second leitmotif of the *Violin Concerto* appears. The remark, "When she is smoking a pipe" corresponds to Bartók's characterization of this motif that portrays the impetuous Stef Geyer–humorous, witty and entertaining.

72 Béla Bartók, *Briefe* (Rákospalota, Mariastrasse 15, August 20, 1907), no. 7, sec. 10.

detail"[73] and which is now illuminated from another perspective by an ingenious Frenchman in support of Bartók's prior discussions and polemics on this topic:

> At 16 years old the teenager knows what it is to suffer, for he has suffered himself. But he hardly knows that other beings also suffer: to see it without feeling it is not to know, and. . ... the child, not imagining what others feel, knows no evil but his own. But when the first awakening of the senses ignites the fire of imagination within himself, he begins to feel with his fellows, to be moved by their complaints, and to suffer from their sorrows. It is only then that the sad picture of suffering humankind must bear in his heart the first tenderness he has ever experienced.[74]

Over a period of a about a week Bartók refined his plans to travel with his mother to Venice on September 1st. He cordially requested a few lines from Stefi to let him know if they might see each other before that and, despite all the rush, "[p]erhaps we could 'regern' once or twice? There are still three unknown *Violin Sonatas* by R. [Reger] (from the Aibl publishing house)." The letter was finally finished and for once signed rather grandiosely: "Be nobly greeted by a certain artist who rejoices if he can 'regern' with you."[75]

Though short-lived, this tale is a love story that is true. It is also worth recounting because the characters who enact it are important–and at least for one of them, had important consequences for his life, and through his life for the history of music.

---

73   Ibid., sec. 11. The wise man quoted here is Jean-Jacques Rousseau and the text shedding light on the question is *Émile*, Bk 4.

74   Béla Bartók, *Briefe*, no. 7, sec. 11.

75   Ibid., sec. 12.

3 Béla and Stefi: Coda of Anguish

In the late summer of 1907, Béla anxiously and eagerly awaited each of Stefi's letters. One of these in August informs us that Stefi's letter had arrived but not yet reached its addressee. Bartók wonders whether it brings good or bad news: "Perhaps you were only going to tell me a few jokes? Or had you something more serious to put on paper? Which part of my letter would you have thought about and commented on? These conjectures gave me such a headache, I had to do something about it as soon as possible."[76] Distress and misery fill his heart. But when Stefi writes to him: "For life is so beautiful! There's so much beauty in nature–the arts–science,"[77] Béla is filled with joy and considers these statements the most exquisite thoughts she has expressed to him so far.

> And why? Because it reflects my own view of life. It is one of man's weaknesses that we only recognize the correctness of judgments when they correspond with our own–a pardonable shortcoming.
>
> I am infinitely grateful to you for your letter just because you put in those 4 or 5 lines which have given me the most intense delight. There may be some interest–even some charm–in exploring a conception of things which is quite alien to one's own. But to come upon a fellow human being–more, a friend–who shares, albeit in a different form, the ideas on which one's whole conception of the world is founded: that is one of the purest joys. It is evident from what you write that you have indeed failed to understand–or rather, you have misunderstood–my words about the lack of a purpose of existence. However, we must talk about that another time.[78]

These sentiments reveal Bartók's aesthetic delight and the intellectual camaraderie he shares with Stefi, and they come close to how he would articulate the meaning of human life. The same letter, however, also introduces a subject that elicits an exchange of thoughts that challenges her beliefs, namely, the issue of God and its relation to the purpose for living.

> Suddenly, after those 4 or 5 delightful lines, you broach [sic] a weighty question such as we have never discussed as yet. But it had already occurred to me that there might come a day when we felt obliged to discuss this subject; and I am truly glad that this time, in contrast to what has always happened so far, the initiative has not had to come from me.[79]

---

76 *Béla Bartók Letters*, Demény, 75.
77 Ibid.
78 Ibid.
79 Ibid., 75–76.

Béla confesses that he too had once been devoted to Christian values and traditional morality. But by the age of 22, he had become a staunch opponent of Christianity and for the last four years considered himself an atheist:

> I was absolutely convinced–although we have never talked about it–that you were "God-fearing." It wasn't difficult for me to put two and two together. This makes it all the more difficult for me to touch on this subject. I am almost afraid to begin.
>
> After giving these matters a great deal of thought, I have–almost in spite of myself–arrived at certain conclusions which may be summed up in the following–*corrected*–biblical assertions.
>
> With amazing consistency, the Bible preaches the contrary of the truths learned in our existence on earth. For it isn't God who created man in his own image, after his likeness: *It is man who created God after his own likeness.* It is not the body that's mortal and the soul that's immortal, but the other way round [sic]: *The soul is transitory and the body (that is, matter) is everlasting!. . .*
>
> In several letters you have mentioned your lack of [religious] experience. Now you plead that you are no philosopher. But what is religion if not pure philosophy?. . .
>
> Therefore, since you have "no experience to speak of," whereas I have some, albeit slight, and since you are "no philosopher" as yet, whereas I have already dabbled in that subject, I hope you will allow me to develop the two axioms I have already stated.[80]

This statement of a young thinker generally acquainted with certain trends in contemporary philosophy, discloses a critical spirit that belies its wholesale acceptance of the common positions in the repertory of late nineteenth-century atheism. If Bartók's portrayal of Stefi is even reasonably on target, then she would not have been able to conclude whether or not his reasoning was original and convincing.[81] His extended argument evinces a committed atheism unwilling to give Stefi's Catholicism any benefit of the doubt since, as his letters have shown, he professes to have long since abandoned the beliefs he once held and emerged an enlightened man. Béla's advocacy of atheism, which he explicitly links to his

---

80 *Béla Bartók Letters*, Demény, 76–77.

81 The rather general and imprecise nature of the arguments advanced by Bartók suggest but cannot confirm what appears to be his reliance on secondary sources rather than primary texts of the great modern philosophers. This is the more likely hypothesis when one considers his age, the context of a life steeped in music, and preoccupied with romance as well as the summary nature of arguments indebted to such diverse and prolific thinkers as Denis Diderot, Ludwig Feuerbach, and Friedrich Nietzsche. However, as we have seen, Bartók indicated that he at least had read Nietzsche. See Michael J. Buckley, *At the Origins of Modern Atheism* (New Haven: Yale University Press, 1987), 145–250; and James Collins, *God in Modern Philosophy* (Chicago: Henry Regnery, 1959), 238–268.

consistently nihilistic worldview, translates into an ideology of life that would most likely be a troubling obstacle for a young woman thinking of love and beginning a career that already for her time involved a fair amount of psychological dislocation.

Though he has concerns about Stefi's reception of his words and fears that she might change the way she feels about him, he prophesies to her that

> [life] on this globe had a beginning at some time; consequently, it is bound to come to an end–at some time. . . . [T]he way in which it happens is irrelevant; what counts is the certainty that it will happen. But before the day of total annihilation, the views, tastes and disposition of the social establishment are bound to be radically transformed. Those things we appreciate highly at the present time will be scorned at a later date, and vice versa.
>
> In a thousand years, in 10 thousand years, I am sure that my whole work will have been lost without a trace; and maybe the entire Hungarian people and their language will have sunk into oblivion forever. Or if not by then–well then, some time [sic] later. The same fate awaits the work of everyone [sic] of us. It would not be a pleasant thing to work with only this depressing thought in mind. To be able to work, one must have a zest for life, i.e. a keen interest in the living universe. One has to be filled with enthusiasm for the Trinity about which you write so eloquently in your letter; if I ever crossed myself, it would signify "In the name of Nature, Art and Science. . ."
>
> Isn't that enough?! Must you have the promised "hereafter" as well? That's something I can't understand.
>
> It's very strange, this making friends by letter. I wonder how we'll get on??![82]

We may find it rather surprising for Bartók to write about these issues while hoping at the same time to deepen his friendship with Stefi. And still he pours it on: "You are 'no philosopher' as yet? Never mind! The important thing is that you should want to become one. You are still green? Never mind! The important thing is that you should want to mature. (You aren't as green as all that!)"[83]

Despite such a perspective, some purpose to life must be found. A person must settle for what is possible, and, for Bartók, this purpose (despite his earlier denials) appears to be recognition, honor, and the comfort to pursue one's own interests:

> That is to say, on a small scale, everybody and every living thing–even mosquitoes and fleas–have an object in life. For instance, as far as I am concerned, it is, on however small a scale, to give a few people some minor pleasures; on a bigger scale, to work for the good of that set of corrupt demi-gentlemen we call the Hungarian intelligentsia by

---

82 *Béla Bartók Letters*, Demény, 82.
83 Ibid.

collecting folk-songs, etc., etc. In return, I am provided with a living, and my name will be included in the next edition of the encyclopedia (so that I may be more get-at-able for all the would-be-academician, patronage-seeking ivory-ticklers that infest this country). The object in life and the reward are equally splendid.[84]

Do Bartók's ironies here provoke the young lady and do his cynical arguments upset her? We can only surmise that Béla leaves her disappointed, and for good reason. His perception of life suggests a young man at once arrogant and insecure, certain and hesitant, brilliant yet sadly naive. This appears most clearly in passages where he feels compelled, in the interest of his love relationship with Stefi, to impress her with philosophical matters. The 26-year-old Bartók, like many Central European intellectuals of his day, was clearly dominated by Nietzsche's ideas, especially his atheism, his exaltation of the individual, the intellectual strength that disdains being affected by trivia, and the spiritual power that rises above everything.[85] "Each must strive to rise above all; nothing must touch him; he must be completely independent, completely indifferent. Only thus can he reconcile himself to death and to the meaninglessness of life."[86] Following Nietzsche, Bartók allows for no compromise in the quest to reach the highest level of existence despite its metaphysical unmooring. The ideal of becoming self-sufficient by means of a carefully developed ethic that is based on common sense, duty, and faculty of judgment can be helpful in the battle against fate.[87] It is this new spirit that will emerge as Bartók's ideal. It is at once absolute and rarely attained. Yet even success here has its disadvantage, for what exists can no longer be an ideal. However, as we shall see, the problem is somewhat academic since Bartók was not always true to his own line of reasoning.

---

84 Ibid.

85 András Batta elucidates the influence of Nietzsche on Bartók's thinking: "Eternity's infinite recurrence is the only fact accepted as truth by Nietzsche. And there is a cause of the nature of that perception. And since the primal matter of the human will exists independently, the eternity idea requires a cold-minded state: the liberation, the purification of human sensations, as Nietzsche says: from the human 'flaws.'" ("Gemeinsames Nietzsche-Symbol bei Bartók und bei R. Strauss" in *Studia Musicologica Academiae Scientiarum Hungaricae*, Budapest, 1982): vol. 24, 281.

86 Letter to Irmy Jurkovics, dated August 15, 1905, in *Béla Bartók Letters*, Demény, 50–51.

87 Bartók was also intrigued by Schopenhauer, whose conception of the will to power anticipates Nietzsche's attempt to overcome a mediocre destiny. See, János Kárpáti, "Early String Quartets," in *The Bartók Companion*, ed. Malcolm Gillies (London: Faber and Faber, 1993), 226.

On the other hand, Stefi, as a young woman steeped in traditional Catholicism, must have found Béla's remarks troubling if not shocking. There is the further obstacle of the pedagogue: Bartók often assumes the role of schoolteacher who is trying to set her on the right path:

> Will you allow me to supply you with reading matter from time to time? (Something not too weighty as a start, just to bring you onto the right track; no middle-of-the-road stuff.) You needn't be afraid that reading will blight your youth; even if it were to shorten it, you would be amply compensated by all the pleasure you would get from it. (Not, of course, that reading ever does shorten youth!) . . . .
>
> I could come round and see you about half-past twelve, Monday, I hope to get away from the Academy by then . . . .
>
> It is one o'clock in the morning. At 6 a.m. I shall be on my way back. It seems I must have come to Vésztő for no other purpose than to intercept your letter and answer it from here.
>
> Think about the "Infinite" and thinking, shudder and bow your head.
>
> > Greetings from
> >
> > AN UNBELIEVER
> >
> > (who is more honest than a great many believers)[88]

By Béla's writing in such a belittling manner, it is not difficult to understand why such arguments caused Stefi to react strongly and immobilized her feelings, at least in the short term. Yet even then he cannot let the matter drop, but falls repeatedly into a patronizing and skeptical attitude, reminding Stefi of the Hungarian expression–*lelkibeteg* ["soul-sick"]–that refers to the mind working poorly until it completely shuts down.[89] The coining of such a phrase, he notes, belies the immortality of the soul. But then a letter arrives with Stefi's response, and Bartók's eyes tear up when he finishes reading it.

> Here is a case of human frailty! I anticipated that you might react like this, yet when you actually did so, I was upset. Why couldn't I read your letter with cold indifference! . . . But when it comes to the idea of the existence of god–which is no less of a supposition–this is put forward as an incontrovertible truth, unquestioned alike by those who invented it and those amongst whom it was propagated. And this in spite of the fact that ordinary common sense tells us that it is a theory full of inherent contradictions and open to all kind of suspicions; as, for instance, the idea that an immortal being can be invested with mortal qualities. . .

---

88 *Béla Bartók Letters*, Demény, 83.
89 Ibid., 87.

> I would never attempt to talk to you out of your faith, distressed though I am by your present state of mind. Come the first moment of crisis, you would relapse, I am sure— Yes, let us drop the subject.[90]

Certainly after the last exchange the subject of faith and belief was indeed dropped.

Yet something else took on meaning and significant expression: Stefi's identity in the means of musical notation. It is in a letter from around mid-September that Bartók notates the nine measures of *Adagio molto* and closes a bracket above the rising four-note motif (C#-E-G#-B#), telling Stefi that this is her leitmotif. "What is to be the end of it all? And when?"[91]

In the letter begun in Rákospalota late on September 16th but finished on the following day at 2:00 a.m. before the "grey hour," Béla announces that he will come to see her as planned on Wednesday at the usual time, even though his schedule has been altered by a major disappointment: "The Philharmonic orchestra does not want to perform my *Serenade* (too bad for the Philharmonic)."[92] He then wonders how long it has been since he has written, calculating that it has been all of six days! He is happy that at the end of his last visit Stefi discreetly acknowledged that she had received his letter. It seems that despite their intense discussion on the topic of religion in their last communication, things were not so bad after all or at least not the worst imaginable. Béla is encouraged with the relaxed mood and concludes jokingly that the next time he comes to visit, it would be with a sack and a pair of pliers in it, and if she would allow, he will try to pull a serious and honest word out of her. "End (so let it be)."[93]

At this time Bartók continued to visit with Stefi at her family's summer home as well as city home. At the same time, he began to jot down the musical ideas that he identified as her leitmotifs in the *Concerto* he is writing for her. During this time, we encounter a vast trove of his expressive thoughts and emotions on the subject of the *Concerto's* genesis and fate. But his letter of September 20, 1907[94] contains an unusual paragraph in which he quotes Stefi's three desired images: the motif of "Love" in the Andante that serves as the quasi-Adagio in the first movement, the "Virtuoso Violinist" in the Allegro giocoso of the second

---

90 *Béla Bartók Letters*, Demény 83–86.

91 Ibid., (September 11, 1907), 87.

92 Béla Bartók, *Briefe an Stefi Geyer*, Rákospalota, 16th of September, to be exact 17th, 1907 (2 a.m.), no. 10, sec. 3.

93 Ibid., sec. 4.

94 Accordingly, we find Lajos Nyikos' comments in *Béla Bartók, Briefe an Stefi Geyer*, p. 212 that his undated letter, written on a Friday must be dated on September 20 and it would refer to Bartók's visit with Stefi Geyer on Wednesday, September 18.

movement, and finally the descending progression that fuses her "Ideal" and "Virtuoso" leitmotif transformations.[95] "Your leitmotifs are buzzing all around me. All day long I live with you, in you, as in a narcotic dream. And this is good; one needs such opium in order to work. It does not matter if it is nerve-racking, even poisonous, and even dangerous."[96]

On the following Sunday morning, Béla is hoping for another visit at Stefi's home in Budapest to pick up some music of Brahms, as well as to receive her comments and suggestions, possibly on the second movement of her *Concerto*.

If you are not at home, then I ask that you leave your suggestions in writing along with the Brahms music for me to pick up. The last time I managed to get out of you what I wanted without a pair of pliers–it was sad enough what I received. More and more despondency is gathering in my poor head. As if a "Great God" were speaking: "You are a miserable and fraudulent mortal; an even more settled fate could befall you; Look! Own it, I'm telling the truth!" And with this I get overpowered with new, unexpected suffering. Since Wednesday I have had great compassion for you, although you do not feel your lack of freedom to the extent I commiserate with you because of it. And so for you all my compassion is infinite, isn't it? But how much of this is not comprehensible when a man is–in the opium rush![97]

A postcard addressed to Miss Stefania Geyer, Ferencring 40, Budapest, September 26th, 1907, follows the letter. We turn our attention to the presence of two themes on the postcard that are placed in the final version of the *Violin Concerto* in the second movement.

---

95 Béla Bartók, *Briefe*, 11.
96 Béla Bartók, *Briefe* (September 20, 1907), no. 11, sec. 1. Prior to this letter Bartók visited with Stefi on September 18th, according to Nyikos' data.
97 Ibid., secs. 2–3.

"As provisions for a journey[98]

2. Movement of the Violin Concerto (toward the end)

a) 4. And 5. bar after 34

b) 4. And 5. bar after 29: a variant of the second leitmotiv"[99]

The significance of this postcard is that of Bartók's reaching out to Stefi with the question of the instrumental settings. For alongside the music, he writes: "How would you score the accompaniment?" And "Which is better?"[100]

Bartók's next postcard of October 14, 1907, addressed to Miss "Stefanchen Geyer, Violin *Virtuoso*, Ferencring 40, Budapest," shows a picture of Rubens' "The Head of Medusa."[101]

> What pleasant gracing! Do you love such an animal society? How cute is that little sal-amander there in the left corner. I would be immeasurably happy if I could enrich the richness of your zoo by populating it with similarly creeping creatures; but the fauna of Rákospalota are so poor! Even the most meticulous excavations cannot begin to bring a gaunt earthworm to light. However, the purpose of my lines is to announce my visit to tomorrow at half past two; I will come to pick up the forgotten-by-you-but-forever-beautiful R. [Reger] and the rest of my books. All of a sudden, I can't drag away the

---

98   Stefi is on the concert tour. Bartók uses both instrumentations in the Second Movement of the *Concerto* (the closing of the second theme group at [Reh. 15] in a'tempo, $\quarternote = 76$ and 5 measures after [Reh. 29], $\halfnote = 54$).

99   Béla Bartók, *Briefe* (September 26, 1907), no. 12.

100 Ibid.

101 Ibid., (October 14, 1907), no. 13. This painting was and remains in the collection of the Kunsthistorisches Museum in Vienna.

heavy stuff after all. If you are not at home, be so kind and leave it there for me. I wish you every bliss![102]

Three more postcards from Nyitra, Slovakia make their way to Stefi on Sunday, October 27th. Two of them are addressed to Fräulein Stefi Geyer,[103] and the second one tenderly employs the diminutive, Fräulein Stefanchen Geyer.[104]

For a month Bartók reflects on his inability to reach Stefi even when he reverts to using quill. In his letter of November 26th, he questions her ability to carry through on correspondence or simple picture postcards. Nyikos comments that Stefi might have dishonored Bartók with a mocking remark on the "leitmotifs address" from his September 20th letter.

> Though worse than an "absolute nothing" can be only a "few" [responses]–I would go for "many" when I have a choice. Given these three possibilities, "few" is what is satisfying you; very often, however, the "golden mean" [is what is needed]. Now about what should I write, if anything at all? You maintain that there is nothing happening out there around you. . . . [T]he situation is certainly not any better here, except in the world of my soul–though this is exactly the spot where the difficulties arise. About what happens inside me, or has already happened, about three-fourths of it I cannot report, as we have agreed upon. In our "inner-world" of thoughts there are forbidden domains that we are not allowed to discuss according to our last exchange of letters.[105]

To summarize, there are two problems here that make Béla unhappy and frustrated: a paucity of personal thoughts and life sharing from Stefi, and a contraction of the number of permitted topics.

Bartók poses a question as to why Stefi did not want him to write while she was traveling to Leipzig and Dresden. For she had insisted that there was to be no correspondence between them, although he later learned that Stefi's mother had written her either daily or every other day. "So there was a way to send you a letter. . . you just did not want any from me."[106] How devastating this must have been for the young lover who wanted to maintain the joy they had experienced during their last two encounters. Frustrated and unhappy, he wondered why those days had been by contrast so warm and friendly. "When you scolded me in

---

102 Ibid. In this context it is a rather skeptical allusion to Stefi's self-righteousness.

103 Ibid., nos. 14 and 16.

104 Ibid., no. 15.

105 Béla Bartók, *Briefe* (November 26, 1907), no. 17, sec. 1. Nyikos informs us that Stefi Geyer was on concert tour through the major German cities of Leipzig, Dresden, and Dortmund.

106 Ibid.

English," he asks, "was this also an expression of politeness or did it come from your heart?" But finally, toward the end of November, a warm postcard arrived from Leipzig that cheered him up:

> And you should know what went through my mind after the first moments of joy: this is all a joke, your hand writing a fake![107] This would have been a cruel joke, one not to be expected from
>
> No! the signature is authentic! However, it was not so much the external gesture that made me so happy, it was the fact that you were thinking about me while being so far away.[108]

Béla clearly needed this assurance and an external sign to restore his happiness. At the very least, it proved to him that Stefi indeed was thinking of him.

Yet, regardless of whether she made him happy or he thought that she treated him cruelly, Bartók feverishly worked on the *Concerto* for her during these emotionally trying weeks of his "grey" November. His frequent quotations of the main leitmotifs in his letters to her show the absolute fusion of his musical thoughts, emotions, and love for her. It must have been the depth of the identity between work and purpose in the spirit of Tristan that would lead Bartók to deny the *Concerto* publication and performance after his relationship with Stefi had ended.[109]

> You lovely, you good, you fairy-like, you enchanting girl! The one from whom only some feather strokes are needed and at once the furious, clenching clouds disappear from the sky and the beaming sun shines on me again. You silent, you angry, you cruel, you ambitious girl! That you use your magical power so sparingly! For you need to know that I have awakened to a cruel, unfriendly morning; through the constant brooding and senseless struggle and almost at the end of my strength, I no longer will complain about anything. Only this tangled thought hammers as an *idée fixe*[110] in my head: nowhere, neither in art nor in friendship, is there any success–only failure![111]

---

107 A joke; Stefi Geyer's card must also have carried Reger's signature.

108 Béla Bartók, *Briefe* (November 29, 1907), no. 18, sec. 1.

109 The denouement will be fully revealed in Chapter 5 of this book.

110 Bartók is acting like Berlioz did to his beloved, Harriet Smithson. She too had rejected him, and so the idée fixe is transformed from the portrait of the beloved into the grotesque theme of the witch.

111 Béla Bartók, *Briefe* (December, 8 1907), no. 20, sec. 1.

But Stefi's letter arrived and all these ill-fated crises of thoughts and emotions were placed on hold. A renewed hope awakened for Bartók "that on the more beautiful, better and friendlier battleground, roses can still be blooming."[112] Still he is not certain about the future; but then, who can be? So he speculates and doubts. Yet if this ideal future spring does come, and the spring time will force its demands, then for sure and only then will a faultless sunshine appear.

> Since then, I have again had minor doubts as to whether I should interpret the dark lines of your letter in a good sense or bad, for such dismal lines were found in rich profusion. And perhaps this is also the reason why I am rewriting against your firm commandment. For what should this sentence mean at the end of your letter, what else can it mean than this very absolute ban: "So it is better; just don't misunderstand this again." But whether I understand it well or poorly, it is still wrong; I don't understand it at all! Why is it better if we don't write to each other? Are you scared for me, are you afraid for yourself, or do you want to save time? I can't imagine it would bore you; otherwise you would not have been gone for such a long time this summer. So why is it supposed to be so much better not to write to each other? [Here in the letters] is the only opportunity for us to be able to speak openly to each other; the spoken word–the serious one–always gets stuck in one's throat–one left for only the speaker to know. And this is also shown by the facts. Or you do not want this candid directness, and that's why it's better if even this unique opportunity is cast aside. But I have to say that a strange quietness is beginning to develop: twists and turns stumbling over ambiguities, corrections and rewrites for everything as if we were trying to call things by their names.[113]

Bartók's personal mood and the atmosphere were varying from day to day, maybe even from one hour to the next, but their object remained the same. Although he has tried to change his disposition and free himself from this emotional dependency, the success of doing so lasted mostly through brief spasms of energy. He would then fall back into the old and familiar surroundings. Stefi's letter, of course, reassured Bartók of the promise of their relationship, and Bartók continued to advance in both his personal hope toward Stefi and the *Concerto's* virtuoso movement.

> Now look! I didn't deserve this ink with the prick of provocative irony! . . . . Composing the second movement I will succeed even more, I think! However, I wish it would be
>
> reversed. . . . No, I cannot separate myself from

112 Ibid.
113 Ibid.

[Stefi's ideal image], even I have tried. Though one does not have to be always 6/8 D-F$^\sharp$-

A-C$^\sharp$, one has to be  sometime.[114]

It is in this letter of December 8th that Bartók goes back to his time in Jászberény in the previous summer when Geyer invited him to join her–a time when much was still up in the air for him: to go or not to go, to let off steam or not. In the summer and autumn, times had been better. Most days then were bright and cheerful, but now everything has changed and, according to Bartók, for the worse. Toward the end of his letter, we find this poignant phrase: "I only would like to know what you do when you are required to listen to something that in reality is of no interest to you. Do you know what the piece means for me? No, you do not know; so I will answer: everything. And for you?"[115]

---

114 Ibid., sec. 5.

115 Béla Bartók, *Briefe* (December 8th), no. 20, sec. 6. The sense of the translated question at the end of this quotation is: "What does it mean for you?" I gave the incorrect date of December 7th to this letter in my article, "Béla Bartók's 1907 Violin Concerto: In the Spirit of Tristan," in the *International Journal of Musicology*, vol. 7 (1998).

4 Béla and Stefi: An Unendurable Farewell

The increasingly foreboding content and tone of the letters prepare us unconsciously for the sad and painful closure between the two correspondents. For they reveal the incommensurate relationship between these two lovers, if they are indeed two–one in which Béla adores Stefi but she holds him at arm's length. And differences of age, education, maturity, and varying stages in their respective careers set up further hurdles. There is the further relative paucity of responses from Stefi. When she does respond, we are rarely privy to her lines, for they have been mostly lost to history. So we must guess, just as Béla for other reasons must too often guess. As a result, in the presence of disguised twists and turns of phrase that displace the speech of pure tone and lucidity, he asks Stefi to write sincerely what she is thinking and feeling. He encourages her to try to define her misgivings in order to preclude the likelihood of misunderstanding, but she appears mostly unable and partly unwilling to recognize the state of their relationship, to explain how and why it is that way.

At least that is what the student of this mostly one-way avenue must conclude: Stefi must have answered Béla's manifold questions and perhaps with seductive lines full of thrilling duplicity and vagueness. For in the following letter of December 11th, he asks her with some intensity to write about serious issues that she has only superficially mentioned in her letter:

> I will spend the Christmas holidays together with my mother at my sister's, then I come back to Pest for three to four days, travel again for a couple of days, then back again. I will then be traveling for my research on the field work. It will thus be a long time before I see you. That's why I ask you to please write again before then and explain what I asked you about: what are those thoughts and feelings that you mostly guess at and intuit? How are they, what do they relate to, are they good or bad, do you want to liberate yourself from them or not? You will do it, won't you?![116]

But this time we know that Stefi did respond to him, but we do not know what she wrote. We can only speculate on the basis of his reactions. Did it express a cruelty arising from her heart? If so, one might hypothesize the reasons for her willingness to injure the young man and incite a deeper cynicism in him. Were these the words of a mature Stefi with full deliberation who led him on and insisted: "No I cannot go with you"? Or those of a mere nineteen-year-old, confused about love's threats and mysteries, that led her to say "not now" but wait

---

116 Béla Bartók, *Briefe an Stefi Geyer* (December 11th), no. 20, sec. 9.

if you can and try to withstand the wait–"sometime later I will go with you; but for now, I must follow my own way"? We further know that the young composer cannot bear her "grey," ambiguous words. Again, he responds in writing since it is too difficult to do so verbally.

1   It is not "anger" that is expressed in [your letter]: it is feminine cruelty that is pervading through you. For it is cruelty to lead someone somewhere and then halfway–on unknown paths–to abandon him. . . .. This is the language of unkindness. But don't let the waiting continue for too long; in the meantime, the string is tightening–until it breaks. Look, just the other day you scolded me because I don't sleep or eat; but your wrath is at least half responsible for this. After such a letter, it might be even worse. How much did I await this letter! Two days ago I dreamt all night about you, and a premonition told me in the morning that today it would come for sure. This premonition was of course wrong! And then when I am thinking that this will continue for months–either nothing or little or "angry"! How can one survive such torment? And you yourself remind me to take care of my health. Under such circumstances this is difficult. I have to be content when I manage somehow, poorly, miserably. With great effort I can come to terms–what else should I do–with the fact that you are delaying the explanation of your mysterious lines, not until hell freezes over [ad calendas graecas] but until you have gotten to know yourself. You trust neither yourself nor me; so let's wait! But I cannot wait for your self-knowledge forever.

2   But that I am supposed to accept without complaint that I'm not allowed even to receive a message from you–that is impossible, you must understand. And I did ask about that, but you did not answer me. Why do you act coy when the talk is about whether or not we should write to each other? What harm could this do? Here I can see only one single circumstance that would speak against it: if it were boring and unpleasant for you, or if you absolutely and categorically and for no other reason did not want the exchange of letters! . . ..

3   I have to return in more detail to a very angry remark in your letter. It is strange how stubbornly you hold on to a misunderstanding after you have taken one of my sentences the wrong way. "Detached." It seems that in my former letter this word made the strongest impression on you since you mention it again and again–of course, always in the sense that you attach to it. It is in vain that I explain by "detachment" that I meant that this feeling no longer gave me pleasure, but only put me in a state of despair. Whether this feeling itself will ever leave me, I don't know; but one thing is certain: that another such feeling will never again take its place. If it should, I will fight against it only in the extreme case and there is no longer any consolation for me. The later I encounter such an extreme case, the more painful will be the fight and the more questionable the result! Before your concert in Budapest I already thought the time had come; I sacrificed everything; I wanted to withdraw myself: your violin concerto would not have happened–only a strange misunderstanding pulled me out of it. But neither do I want to talk about this anymore now nor bore you with it.

4 And that you could write: "I can't say it, at most down the road–when

will vanish completely! In any case it will not last

long–at least we hope so for your benefit." No, and a thousand times no, you did not need to write that. If you are already *cross*,[117] you should at least be honest. So you really *hope* this; you really believe that you could first say that to me after such an unfortunate change of heart. Such could only happen (if at all) if I were not to see you for years, nor write you, nor engage you in any way whatsoever; but amazingly by that very fact you could then not say that [under those circumstances].

5 No! You must take that back if you want to be honest. But if this would be in fact your actual thinking–then that once again means for me the extreme case mentioned above.
Final conclusion: you want to torment me by leaving me in suspense for a time. You may have well-grounded reasons for this; I resign myself to this. But only for a time. Longer is really not possible.

6 But why do you want to make this misfortune yet complete by depriving me of a letter for weeks, for months; this I do not understand. Isn't it true that you would not do that? You would not begin your letter with the stereotypical phrase, "I don't have much time for writing," "I didn't have time, I couldn't write." I know in any case that you indeed had time. In other cases you write on a daily basis. From this time taken you could devote a little of it to me. For the world would not come to an end if you were then to write only 24 pages a week instead of 28; but these four pages would mean the world to me.

7 I would very much like to request that you send me at least the bare minimum of lines on how and where you spent Christmas Eve; that would not require hardly any time at all.[118]

From 9:00 p.m. in the evening until 6:00 a.m. on the morning of December 24th, Bartók was working uninterruptedly on finishing the *Concerto*, partly taking it out of sketches with some parts still in pencil in order to have it ready for Stefi to look at it before Christmas and for him to be able to share it as a Christmas celebration and personal gift.[119] "Will you like it? Will you accept it? . . . .it speaks only and alone about you and to you. This one I really wrote 'with my soul,' and

---

117 Here Bartók's use of the English word "cross" is placed in italics to show how he reaches into another language, probably for emphasis.

118 Béla Bartók, *Briefer* (December 21, 1907), no. 21, secs. 1–7.

119 We know that officially the manuscript was finished on February 5, 1908 and that Stefi received it 11 days later according to the posted dates by Bartók on the first and last pages of the manuscript.

what do I care if nobody will like it; only you have to like it."[120] He concludes by stating his wish to see her and hopes to have this opportunity soon.

Bartók's 1908 diary notes of January 7th, 9th, and 14th lay bare some critical thoughts and powerful feelings about a musical event both he and Stefi attended:

> Yesterday was the concert of the "Wiener-Quartet."[121] What a great day for me! As long as I live, particular measures of this quartet will remind me of the unimaginable contrasting emotions I lived through yesterday. During the last half year–starting at the end of June–I have experienced some truly critical days, and nearly each time I thought: this is the biggest crisis of all. Now there can be only total collapse or improvement. No! I only thought of collapse! And look, yesterday exceeded everything else till then. I went through all the phases of hope, doubt, despair–finally, after a drop of happiness, to fall back into assumptions; what else is there for me? In the morning I was still hoping. I was waiting for some kind of wonder that might happen during my visit in the afternoon and that might somehow resolve my wretchedly desperate situation.[122]

From the same diary notes we know that Bartók was sitting not far from Geyer and that he was looking at her anxiously and furtively–"she was so beautiful"–[123] as he had never seen her before. During the entire concert, Béla admitted that he hardly knew what was happening around him. He had such a heartthrob that "it was a miracle nothing serious happened to me."[124] Stefi, however, appeared to be unaware of what was transpiring inside Bartók's soul. His face was providing cover like that of a skilled actor who can hide everything. But the agony of undergoing such a spiritual struggle that must remain hidden is known only by those who have experienced it. To explain it is impossible, Béla concedes.

In the course of the evening it came to the irrevocable last handshake, the last farewell word in Bartók's thoughts "forever." Instinctively, he followed her and let all of his acquaintances stand waiting, for he felt that the two of them had to speak a few last words to each other. While her father was chatting to an acquaintance, Béla and Stefi walked off together, but mostly silent. Béla later reflected on their conversation in one of his diary entries:

---

120 Béla Bartók, *Briefe* (December 23, 1907), 57.

121 "Wiener Quartet," The Joachim String Quartet in residence in Berlin in 1869–1907 was famous for performing all sixteen Beethoven quartets on tour through such major cities of Europe as Bonn, Rome, London, and Vienna. Quartet No. 14 (C♯ minor, Op. 131) was especially popular and devotedly attended since it successfully brought out the greatness of both the composer and the artists.

122 Béla Bartók, *Briefe* (January 7, 1908), an entry from the diary notes, sec. 1.

123 Ibid., sec. 3.

124 Ibid.

Why were you so angry on Saturday? [Stefi's question to Bartók in the course of the evening.] Bitterness fiercely strangled my throat; I could hardly speak out in what could be described as words. And yet, so much did I wish to explain in this brief moment that I was not angry, but I could not disguise my despair; that I was afraid of the coming months, in which we will not even be able to write to each other; how painful it was to be permitted to see you so seldom over Christmas; what has become out of my beautiful plans; the closer the moment of separation came–that Saturday,[125] which I thought was the last one at the time–the less I could control myself. For all this, I could hardly say even a few words.[126]

Béla then records in his diary that Stefi said: "I'm pleased that I wasn't the cause of your bad mood."

She calls that a "bad mood!" Didn't she see my most extraordinary despair, or maybe she didn't want to see it? At the time, I believed that she had seen it, and that this is also why she invited me for the following Monday so as not to let me depart within such a state of soul. In order to prolong my time with her, I went down to the underground railway station. I have never looked more joyfully at the red circle indicating that the train has just departed than I did now. So we had a few more minutes together. While her father was punching the ticket, I looked her in the eyes and allowed myself to gather all my thoughts, all my powers, all my oppressiveness into this one glance–and she returned my gaze. What an unspeakable joy! I don't know how long this rapport lasted. This is the first time we have looked ourselves in the eyes for a long time. This gaze of her eyes will be my only consolation, my sanctuary, my all and everything during the long solitude of her absence.[127]

But if Bartók was looking for a single straw to cling to in his deepest despair and rejection, he found none. The underground train station was his "truthful church."[128] Like a faithful believer returning to the shrine, Bartók returned inwardly to the place where he could embrace the feeling of her presence. His intensified work made it possible for him to endure the following weeks of grief and sadness. And since he was not allowed to write to Stefi, he compressed

---

125 The last encounter mentioned in this letter by Béla Bartók on Saturday, January 4, 1908 was in fact not their absolutely final separation. They saw each other during the Wiener Quartet concert (mentioned above) on the following Monday. On the following day, January 7th, Stefi Geyer traveled to Vienna and then continued on her concert tour until February.

126 Béla Bartók, *Briefe* (January 7, 1908), an entry from the diary notes, sec. 4.

127 Ibid., sec. 5.

128 Bartók's expression in his diary notes of January 7th, 1908 (one day after the concert), sec. 6.

all of these powerful emotions into the pages of his diary notes with her as its addressee. "Will she ever be able to read it?"[129]

As Bartók continued to reveal through his January 1908 diary entries, he felt his heart being truly broken after seeing her and then returning home. Only one thought governed his mind: "All is in vain, even my last hope I shall have to renounce!"[130] Based on their last encounters, it had become obvious to him that there was not even one sliver of hope that might give him any cause for consolation. Although we do not discover a clear motive on her part to break the personal relationship, Stefi's last letter brings nothing other than an honest "setting it right."[131] Bartók interprets this as an interim consolation that, however, does not allow an exit from his unfortunate situation. "No! I've seen it, it can't go on like this. Your parents don't like to see me either, and for you too, it does not matter whether I come or not. At least it appears that way. As a final and conclusive farewell word, I wrote you a desperate letter–which I have written to no one before."[132] On January 9th, 1908 his diary entry was following Stefi's travel schedule:

> She is now in Vienna, in the afternoon she performed at the Salon of I don't know who, and the evening she is certainly spending with that blond youngster who is allowed to be with her much more than I am. He was already in the opera, maybe he went for a walk with her, drove away with her. . ... Yesterday I slept uneasily–in the early morning I awoke. She must have already gotten up, in about an hour she will be in Budapest.[[133]] While I'm writing these lines, she is moving even further away from me–she moves away first toward Innsbruck, tomorrow night she plays there, then. . ... I don't know when she is going where. What cruelty! According to her opinion, "this is better!"[134]

But once again Béla's heart races when an envelope arrives from Stefi. He anxiously opens it. While he was expecting only a violin part and likely nothing personal, he did receive a few simple words at the end that gave him some consolation: "Goodbye. See you in February! And until then all the best. With greetings."[135] Basel was Stefi's next stop and so the next opportunity to send a

---

129 Béla Bartók, *Briefe* (January 7, 1908), an entry from the diary notes, secs. 1–6.

130 Ibid., sec. 2.

131 Ibid.

132 Ibid.

133 Bartók meant to write "Vienna," for according to his notes from January 9th (no. 23, sec. 7) Stefi was on her way to Vienna on that day.

134 Bartók's entry from the diary notes (January 9, 1908), secs. 7–9.

135 Ibid., sec. 9.

postcard to Béla. In the meantime Bartók was working with such feverish haste (or "American fever," as he refers to it) that he "only takes up my little poor diary on rare occasions. Nevertheless, if [I] could write to her, it would be different; for that I would find time despite all!"[136]

On January 30th, Bartók responded to Stefi's correspondence from Vienna with a tragic statement:

> You send me your address. . .for what reason?!

> 1 So, you expect an answer from me?! From one whom you have forbidden–in violation of his own heart–to write to you? As long as I am not allowed to reply to your Christmas letter, I am not in a position to write about anything. But once I have replied, it will either be my last letter to you or simply—.
> It cannot continue on like this; this I am also saying. One has to choose. . .I can't send you anything but unending sadness, bitter renunciation. . .what is the point of writing you? Do you want to feast on my pain? Because I'm not allowed to write, I say everything in the music instead. . .
> 2 The enclosed page is a faithful mirror of my present state of soul.[137] I am sending this to you while trembling; perhaps you will understand it neither as music nor as personal relationship–this is how far I have come! Is there then no living creature on earth that can understand what I want to say!? My God, all this crushing infinite loneliness!
> Indeed I could have even rejoiced that you had made this glowing theme

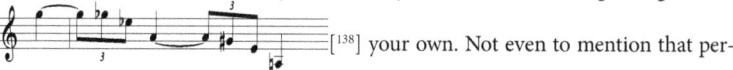

> [138] your own. Not even to mention that per-
> haps you could understand it differently from the way I do. Now I see in it only straw, like leftover straw that you have handed me in my agony of death.[139] I collected this as if it were gems, I beheld them with a diminishing gaze, but not a single one will sprout into a branch of hope. . .So it cannot go on like this.[140]

---

136 Bartók's entry from the diary notes (January 14, 1908), sec. 10.

137 Based on Nyikos' records [77] we can conclude that this is music from Bartók's *Elegy for Piano*, op. 8, no. 1, which he himself dated to February 1908 and which was built entirely on the main thematic idea of the *Concerto*.

138 Béla Bartók, *Briefe*, no. 11, sec.1. The glowing theme (Allegretto) is one of the three "buzzing motifs" of Stefi quoted by Bartók and disclosed to her in his letter of September 20, 1908.

139 The slow theme of the second *Ten Easy Piano Pieces*, the dedication of which is based on the first ideal leitmotif of Stefi.

140 Béla Bartók, *Briefe*, no. 24, secs. 1–2.

On February 8th, 1908 Béla Bartók wrote his last letter to Stefi Geyer, declaring his farewell and taking his leave forever. It is also in this letter that he expressed his declaration of love for the first time. He uses the simple phrase: "I love[d] you" without any mysterious circumlocutions.[141]

1   For the last time! Aren't these words only fitting for someone who prepares for his death? Yet I cannot do it–I still have some obligations. Why did you take leave from me for the last time, then, on Monday evening, with such a long look in your eyes, twice, one after the other–this also I have misinterpreted what I have seen there in your eyes–a sign of encouragement–for quite some time. . . .

2   Actually, this letter is superfluous because I have received from your writing what I wanted: certainty. In it one indeed can no longer interpret anything in a good sense; from it sounds only the last judgment on me. Even though you do not speak out often, you let me feel that you do not have the same feelings toward me as I have toward you–that the relationship between us cannot be the one that would make me happy, that in the best case "it will go on being as it was, perhaps with a slight, barely perceptible difference." And this is, "what I cannot go with anymore." Because you cannot return your feelings in a similar way to what I feel passionately toward you and so my position is hopeless, therefore I will never and can never see you again. I have to try to bury my memories of you forever. . . I have to fight against this en-forced decision; in any event, I could already see by the end of October that every-thing was in vain. Several times already I wanted to break up; why did you hold me back? You did not yet understand what this *Violin Concerto* means to me–the First Movement–*which is my confession to you.* If you understood my feelings in it, why would you then ask so many questions about it? Indeed, I saw that this confession has no effect on you, and this is why I wanted to break up. Before your concert in Budapest[[142]]–when I was cross-examined in your judgement, in truth, I was des-perate. Based on an unhappy misunderstanding, we had agreed that I would look for you after the concert. At that time you were much more friendly to me as you had been in earlier times, and this is why the breaking off could not take place. By the way, this is still nothing. But why did you write your Dortmund letter? Why did you insinuate so much in this letter about you and your hardly known feelings, all kinds of vagueness, and all this as the response to my last letter? If you had not written such a letter at that time, you would have spared me many sufferings and hardships because breaking off then would have been much easier. For at that time I did not *love* you so much as I did after that time–how can I take all of this now? I cannot help myself. That letter from Dortmund was the first letter that revived my hopes. Do you understand correctly: until then . . . this letter, even more specifically, its several hints.

141 Ibid., no. 25, sec. 2.
142 See the reference above in Béla Bartók's Letter, no. 21, sec. 3.

3 My situation, therefore, would be one hundred times easier if I did not have to bring myself down to earth again after such deceptive hopes. Soon after this, you received my particularly impatient letter in which I asked you for assurance.[143] Why did you not give me that certainty then; why did you wait until now? On January 4th I wanted once again to take my leave forever–this is why I appeared so cross-examining, as was your impression–but in truth, sad. After I was rejuvenated, you invited me on Monday. Forty-eight hours of postponement! On the same Monday I returned from you with the greatest doubt and desperation, and right before the concert I wrote a farewell letter to you. I took it with me and after the concert you started to talk to me again in that special way! And by taking leave you looked into my eyes in such way as never before. So, I decided not to send my letter already written to you. Your parting look was my happiness and fulfillment for the next ten days until the doubts came once again. To get to the point, this has been a constant three-month, ongoing cruel torture. Why didn't you execute me with a single blow?! I would have to consider you heartless, if I did not find this so hard, and so I try to attribute this to all kinds of misunderstandings, to find an explanation for your having tormented me so. Perhaps you misunderstood my words from June, my own views on breakup, separation, divorce in marriage in spite of many clarifications I had written about it. Actually, it is not perhaps, but surely the case. Your Christmas letter proves it. In this matter I have never contradicted myself. What I maintained at that time later culminated in a philosophic and legal conviction according to which it is immoral when spouses who do not love each other, but a third person, still have to stay together. However, this does not prove that such a case must necessarily occur; second, it does not follow, for example, that I, because of my philosophic conviction, would intend to marry someone and then after a few years separate again. If someone were to read my words in this way–and I spoke very seriously about this topic–then generally it is both petty and a pity that such a person had misunderstood everything I said. At that time I objected to only one particular lie, which very often is pressed upon many spouses who stand under the pressure and power of marriage vows as well as public opinion. And today it is still my opinion that that the commonly held opinion is extremely immoral.[144]

Apparently Bartók would have to include Stefi among those who misunderstood him, perhaps believing that he could not have any serious intention toward her, and that consequently their relationship did not require any caution or care on her side. This would be a partial explanation for her way of acting. But Bartók doubts that this is sufficient to explain her letter from Dortmund. Was he clear this time? How deeply will he express himself to her? He clarifies: "When I received your letter from Dortmund, I believed that you loved me despite everything and that

143 The impatient letter is Béla Bartók's letter no. 21 of December 21, 1907.
144 Béla Bartók, *Briefe*, no. 25, secs. 1–3.

you could and would be my wife; . . . however, now I know that there is no truth in any of that–you know the rest."[145] And we too know the rest, we who have read the letters, and we who have played the *Concerto*.

Bartók pledges to Geyer not to feel sorry for himself. He announces that he will neither be looking for friends nor writing letters because there is no point in doing so. There is nothing better and no greater benefit than simply to have more time to teach. He is determined to take as many teaching hours "as there are out there," for this occupation will cost him much pain, sorrow, worry, talent, everything. "Everything into dust and nothing. . .My supposition, that I cannot love any other woman than you has provoked your spiteful comments. I have to respond to them with a confession–[inscribed] in my life. . ."[146] Bartók's text brings the reader to silence since it reads as a personal confession of sorts. In the end he admits that he has failed his vows. He had wanted to be faithful to his old pledge to Nietzsche's superiority principal, but then

> I found you. . . .. I arrived at the furthest boundary on the other side of which I cannot ask for the love of anyone else. . .. I feel it. . .. I am forced to give up my inner happiness forever. . .. Perhaps due to some charitable pneumonia or something similar there is a possibility that would allow me to leave quietly the place from which there is nothing more to expect. . ..
>
> I still have a few farewell wishes. You cannot refuse them–for a dying person who requests this of you. Isn't it true, this request you–this is really crazy, but so long as I have not received a firm explanation from you that everything between us is finished, so long as a glimmer of hope continues to revive in my dumber moments–isn't it true that you will explain to me what you were driving at in your letter from Dortmund, why you wrote those words alluding to "unknown feelings?" Why did I receive such an expressive farewell look on January 6th? I cannot find a decent explanation for that, and so I have to see you as a cruel and hard-hearted person; but I still want to remember you as good and innocent. I beg you not to delay this last letter to me. Please do consider it as your last writing to me and how much I am looking forward to these last words from you. On Wednesday you will receive this letter;[[147]] on Friday–morning at the latest–your answer should reach me.
>
> 7   But if everything really is to come to an end–no, this cannot happen, perhaps this should not be the end; just at this moment I have read through your letter again (god knows how many times I have read this already); perhaps it is not totally shattered.[148]

---

145 Ibid., sec. 4.
146 Ibid., sec. 5.
147 By then Stefi will have returned home from her concert tour.
148 Béla Bartók, *Briefe*, no. 25, secs. 5 and 7.

Bartók points to a significant line in Stefi's letter: "It will be as it was, with a slight, almost imperceptible, difference."[149] He speculates about whether this is due to particular conditions that are present at this very moment or for a short time. However, Bartók does not understand why Stefi is playing naïve. He points out the lines she wrote in response to his letter: "lots of talk about all of it and endlessly, only the name is missing."[150] He likewise remembers his own explanation written to her about her feelings and their mutual feelings in the past. And he mentions once again the fact of his having declared to Stefi that he cannot continue to see her if his position in the end is hopeless. But Bartók cannot understand why Stefi is incapable of being specific about her own feelings: "I simply cannot understand why you cannot say something definitive about your own feelings. This is impossible: something cannot develop over a period of years, and then be decided [against] in one or two months. Why do you leave me therefore in this constant uncertainty? [You write]: 'then when I know something, I will let you know.' You must indeed have known something certain back then. Why, why, and again why didn't you decide earlier?"[151] The present question is whether Stefi sees the illogic of her uncertainty. Has she not recognized her own emotional state; has she forgotten the words that meant a world to him? Perhaps Stefi is somewhat to blame for Béla's confusion. So, he decides to send her his diary that contains the notes of the entire week as proof for her to be astounded by and appealed to. "My body would not endure the constant excitement, it would be impossible for me to carry out my daily work, in short it would be not only a mental, but a physical impossibility. That is why I have to ask the question so excessively. And I still hope. . ."[152] And he holds out hope:

> For everything I ask you, don't write me in a mocking tone; but openly speak out the truth as it is, however devastating it may be . . . I must know the truth. My God! How am I going to bear this! Why did all this have to happen?! Five days to go—
>
> Do you see that when you don't write often, how differently I am able to understand your letter; before I saw everything as completely hopeless, and now it is different again.
>
> So I am greeting you for the last time?
>
> Am I really taking leave of you forever?
>
> For the last time?!
>
> Don't be angry about anything; I was partly beside myself when I wrote that.

---

149 Ibid., sec. 7.
150 Béla Bartók, *Briefe*, no. 25, sec. 7.
151 Ibid.
152 Ibid., secs. 7 and 8.

What has happened to my beautiful plans?
Your Dortmund letter
My concealed treasure
My jewel—
Why?

Jesus said to his disciples: "Follow after me, leave behind your parents, acquaintances, relatives." Why isn't it possible that your Jesus be [instead] the sacred thing, the higher duty, the vitality of life?! In view of the higher purpose, why can't you leave behind all these many old traditions?! This leaving behind is no sin, no lack of love. . .I love and honor my mother, and yet I'm supposed to leave her behind–even though I live with her. But no one is able do this–do you know how someone can love and honor, live with, and yet leave behind another–and all this at once and at the same time! Now I feel unburdened, as if I could live despite it all. . .[153]

We speculate that the last letter to Stefi was sent after the manuscript reached its dedicatee. Having been in constant emotional anguish for weeks, Bartók struggled to gather his thoughts and bring clarity and order into the recent events. He recognizes on behalf of them both that it was his strong belief that she loved him. Without any doubt his perception was based on both Stefi's last letter to him as well as her recent behavior. "I am not mistaken. . .please do not deny this."[154] In his last letter of February 1908, undated, he acknowledges that

I can't awaken in myself any joy with this clarity: now I also know that we are both suffering. We are cruelly tormenting ourselves–why–for nothing–because of a false perception–because of your fear that we are incompatible with each other and so would make ourselves unhappy. I am not talking about myself at all; since the beginning of February I have wished for nothing less than to go on living like this [painful relationship]. But you! You can't free yourself from reminiscing of me, you as well are always thinking of me–tormented, your heart is grieving because of me, anguish fills your heart. A single sentence would be enough to prove this clearly: "Now it's going to be a year (since we gotten to know each other)." How often have I thought of this sad, imminent anniversary–because I cannot forget you, for I still love you the same as before. And you therefore think of me too because you still love me. These eight to ten words on Thursday–they said it with full trepidation–your expression in the evening–no indifferent human soul looks like that; in such circumstances no indifferent feeling speaks like that. My God, why do we have to suffer and torment ourselves so! And why should we have to?! I can find no beautiful and appropriate words to express what I feel. In vain

153 Béla Bartók, *Briefe an Stefi Geyer*, no. 26. Editor's note: "Rough and tattered undated octavo page. The thoughts hurriedly strewn here are taken up in the next letter, which is [Bartók's] last, no. 27. For this reason the page is inserted here."
154 Béla Bartók, *Briefe*, no. 27 (Bartók's last letter), sec. 1.

do I want to set much down on paper that I now feel. For the sake of everything I ask you, listen to me–don't push me away–read this to the end.[155]

These lines reveal Bartók's unconditional love toward Stefi. He loves her the way she is, the way he has known her from the start, and absolutely in no other way. It is the remembrance of this Stefi that Béla promises to have and to hold in his heart. "Therefore I am sending you the score because I believe you still love me. . . .I feel it, I would still have much to say to the world–if an anxious interpretation were to bring my word to silence–help me–for all the world."[156] Yet, Stefi's soul was not aligned with Béla's in his act of laying bare feelings of silence and guilt that at the same time shattered the delusion of their intimacy even as he insisted on how things should be between them. Since who they are is revealed in their acts and Stefi is simply incapable of reciprocated love, Béla's love, like his score sent off to her, can never arrive. On the last two pages at the end of the manuscript of the [1907] Violin Concerto, Bartók placed an epigraph: "But even this was a futile battle; a futile strong will, a futile everything."[157] On the first page he wrote:

My confession[158]
For Stefi
still from happy times.
But even that was only part happiness. . .
I.
(Violo solo. . .)   Bartók, Béla
(Score, 30/31. Page, until the last bar)
(In vain, in vain, this poem fell into my hands, there is no consolation for me)[159]

The end.

But not yet. . . The seeming reluctance to rest in this new-found quietude is broken by an impetuous rush to the final coda. The three parts taken in the

---

155 Ibid., sec. 2. In his notes, Lajos Nyikos states [89] that this undated letter was certainly written after the entry of the poem on the last page of the score.
156 Béla Bartók, Briefe, no. 27, sec. 7.
157 These are the words of Béla Balázs, a longtime friend of Béla Bartók. Nyikos explains [90] that the legend holds that Bartók, finding this poem on Zoltan Kodaly's piano, took it with the remark: "That is what I need." The few lines he underscored and chose found their way into the manuscript.
158 Béla Bartók, Briefe, no. 25, sec. 2. In this letter Bartók asks Stefi whether she truly understands what this Violin Concerto means to him. He calls the First Movement his confession to her.
159 Ibid., no. 28.

order of Balázs' poem–Solo, Choir, and Solo–found their voices resounding on the final pages of the *Concerto* manuscript. The last Solo section, which Bartók quotes on the last page, concludes this love story.

> My heart bleeds and my soul is ill:
> I dwelt among mortals.
> I loved with agony, with ardent *love*–
> In vain, in vain!
>
> Your lamb demurs, does it not, you don't understand it,
> Siblings? Siblings?
> No star is so distant from the other star
> As two human souls![160]

In the estate of Stefi Geyer were found the first and last pages of what Bartók called simply the "violin part," which in fact was the single solo part of the *Violin Concerto* dedicated to her. On the first page of this violin part he had written the following sentences in pencil: "Yes, it was you looking back at me from the first floor tonight–you went up there to be happy; I, on the contrary, had a terrible night. Why did I have to go to that concert?" On the last page were the words of the poet quoted by Bartók but written in pencil by Stefi. And underneath was her response in one word: "Verzeihung!"[161]

---

160 Béla Bartók, *Briefe an Stefi Geyer* (16 February 1908), 70; the last Solo section of Béla Balázs' poem.

161 "Forgive me!" The date of Bartók's apparently desperate remark in the context of offering this violin part and score to Stefi cannot be established (Nyikos' Notes [73]).

5 Béla and Stefi: In the Spirit of Tristan

It is the spirit of the Wagnerian Tristan that shows the full significance of the *Concerto* and the episode that inspired it. In the tradition of Romantic self-expression, the spirit of Tristan inspires Bartók to compose this work as an outpouring of unrequited love within a wider exploration of an intense emotional world. Much like Tristan's pursuit of Isolde, Bartók expressed his love and transformed his intention into a musical deed and artifact in the *1907 Concerto*. This work reveals how Bartók's acknowledged enthusiasm for Wagner's chromatic *Tristan* idiom affected his musical thought at this turning point in his career. And the lyrical content of the great opera provided a symbolic content for his own relationship to a beloved who was always so close and yet so far away. Here the Wagnerian unity of story and structure is recapitulated in another composer's life and work: the sounding paean to unrequited love of Wagner's protagonist and the Tristan-like motif with its variants and transformations in fact symbolize two ideals of Stefi Geyer. The polarity, linked by the first hint of the second major motif of the *Concerto*–the *Tristan* grief (or anguish) motif (A-F-E; the yearning leap of the minor sixth)–is projected into the contrasting thematic ideas of the First and Second Movements of the *Concerto*. The *Tristan* leitmotif thus plays a second role as catalyst for taking us from the pole of the ideal-romantic world of Béla and Stefi to the pentatonic-modal world of the peasant, which is also the world of his experience as budding musicologist.

Two of Bartók's letters of November 26th and 29th, 1907 provide the one and only revelation of the meaning of another leitmotif, the major-seventh chord (D-F#-A-C#), which the composer designated as the love-motif for Stefi. By his own testimony, this leitmotif in the *1907 Concerto* signifies a portrait of the young woman, his beloved, in its two opposing presentations: idealized and virtuoso. Both this *Stefi-Isolde* love-motif and the *Béla-Tristan* grief-motif are conveyed through the music in an organic process under numerous metamorphoses and characterizations.

Writing his letters to Stefi Geyer and working on his *Concerto* for her became a simultaneous preoccupation for Béla Bartók. In a letter of September 11, 1907, the composer wrote: "By the time I had finished reading your letter, I was almost in tears–and that, as you can imagine, does not usually happen to me every day."[162]

---

162 *Béla Bartók Letters*, Demény, 83. Stefi's correspondence is not extant, but we assume that her response to Béla's letter of 6 September was critical and upsetting to him.

Although his tears were true and deeply felt, Bartók perceived his own reaction as a display of human weakness. It is also in this letter, in the saddest sentence of all, that we may discern the meaning his despair had for his life and work: "After reading your letter, I sat down to the piano–I have a sad misgiving that I shall never find any consolation in life save in music."[163] And yet music, as Bartók himself recognized, is not a world set apart or an escape to an island of pure forms. Like every art shaped by the human mind, it either expresses something more fundamental than itself, or it turns in on itself and becomes an empty gong, a clashing cymbal. Bartók's *Concerto* is specifically saved from a solipsistic fate as his remark immediately

following reveals: "And yet–this is your 'leitmotiv' "[164]

Since it was not the young composer's predisposition to share the joys and sorrows of his life, and only rarely with the woman he loved, he consorted with music.[165]

It is the late-Romantic idiom of Wagner and Strauss, especially that of *Tristan*, which delivers the concentrated essence of the compositional embodiment of the *Andante*, the *Concerto's* first movement. The passion of frustrated love and the seeming reluctance of the lovers to leave one another are interrupted by a mad rush toward the end. And it is in the *Concerto* itself where we can find the result of that path that leads from the idealized "romantic" world of Stefi to the real and unique world of the peasant. As stated earlier, it is the spirit of Tristan that bridges the gap between both worlds–and yet, as manifested in the concrete musical details of the *Concerto* score, more than just this spirit.

The embodied meaning of Stefi's leitmotifs in Bartók's life and work is revealed and documented in his correspondence with her. But there was a time around October 1907, for a period of more than a month, during which Béla was unable to engage Stefi by means of correspondence except with one very significant exception–that of the *Concerto* score. During this month, a period of both contentment and concern, Béla's work on his *Concerto* became the vehicle of remaining emotionally in touch with her. But then on November 26th, he questioned her

---

163 Ibid., (September 11, 1907), 86–87.

164 *Béla Bartók Letters*, 87.

165 Carl Dahlhaus, in his work *Between Romanticism and Modernism* (Berkeley and Los Angeles: University of California Press, 1980), trans. Mary Whittall, 30, 112 examines the relation of will, feelings, and the musical relation of them in both romanticism and realism.

as to why she had treated him so warmly at their last meeting, presumably in September, although they had been struggling with numerous problems in their relationship. Nevertheless, his previous uncertainty regarding Stefi's feelings for him now seemed less intense. At least, the self-assured yet deeply hurt young disciple of Nietzsche professes to have overcome his emotional difficulties.

> However, I wanted so much to write to you still from Tolna[166] in this mood in my soul occasioned by our last two encounters, which I would have been able to keep up for a long time if you had not knocked me down with the *non possumus*. Immediately I wanted to ask you in writing what was the true reason in our last encounter for your being so friendly (your English rebukes were so dear and lovely) as you had not been since the beginning of September. Was this kind of politeness from you, or did it come from your heart? Because if this is the case; then I would explain with a deep psychoanalysis why I was "upset" sometimes. But look; all that is gone now. Since then the
>
> mood of "  " is melted and has been removed, and
>
> what if left is only a frightened skeleton of the foggy-grey reality. What lonesomeness has settled on me. And the worst is that all of this has crept into my letter and I cannot do anything to fight against it (because I am too weak).[167]

How terrible this must have been for the young man in love who wanted to retain the happiness he had experienced with Stefi during their last encounter. He wishes for this connection to remain; he needs such an external sign to keep his soul warmer and to hold onto his happiness a little longer. As described in the letter above, the "foggy-grey reality" threatens the sensitive Béla as he enters into the slavery of despair. This is the world he now experiences: quagmire competing with wasteland, indifference mirrored in dullness. "I looked at everything from the very beginning as hopeless, and yet I went after it blindly because I couldn't stand this grim, unrelenting grey anymore...Who knows–I thought–perhaps I will become a new feeling and will even be able to create something different, something new."[168] Beginning in July, Béla had gone through extreme and multiple inner modifications of his exhausted soul. For a time, there was hope for a rebirth of his ability to feel and for a rekindling of his desire to create something new through his relationship with Stefi. But it did not last long. Frustrated, unhappy, and wondering about the danger of "getting over" it all, he set out to conquer these crises and become an advocate of a natural indifference. This

---

166 A territory in southwestern Hungary.
167 Béla Bartók, *Briefe an Stefi Geyer,* no. 17, sec. 2.
168 Ibid.

indifference he would embrace until it gradually moved him toward the death that would liberate him.

Bartók reflected on the authentic bond that had existed between Stefi and himself since the summer of 1907 in Jászberény, but which began to be threatened as early as the autumn of that same year.[169] In spite of the uncertainties of their relationship, however, its musical result remained secure. The composer confirms this with respect to Stefi's motif: "This is where I did not betray myself."[170] Music becomes his only comfort and the strength of its language eclipses the paltry medium of its verbal counterpart. The major-seventh-chord configuration of Stefi's leitmotif becomes the very symbol of the depth of his love and passion. Never had he written music like this before. The musical image of the ideal Stefi that is imprisoned in the ascending motif took in all those thoughts and feelings at the time.

> I have never written such direct and personal music like the one you have heard on a memorable day and the music you received with such frostiness and objectivity–just as you will probably take this letter while reading it to the end. And in what a stupid way I imagined the prelude in advance–and then nothing came of it. But what is this outburst of honesty supposed to be? It could only be unpleasant to you and of no help to me either. Would you please honestly tell me if you do not wish to receive such explanations, and I will also place this under the forbidden.[171]

Now we look back and glean that Béla seems to have known already toward the beginning of his friendship with Stefi that all was hopeless, yet he instinctively was hoping against hope or hoping for some resolution–a next step, either a confirmation of her love or an ending of the relationship. If these two individuals are identified with *Tristan* and *Isolde*, one can foresee the tragic doom, the unrequited love engraved in Wagner's *Liebestod*. The weight of Bartók's experience of unrequited love is reflected in his eventual transformation of Stefi's "happy" and "impetuous" leitmotif that opens the second movement of the *Concerto* into the funereal first-movement theme–mourning Stefi's loss–of his *First String Quartet* (1907–1909). [**Ex. 1**]

---

169 They had spent several days of this summer together at the country home of Stefi's relatives.

170 Béla Bartók, *Briefe*, no. 17, sec. 3.

171 Ibid.

Example 1a *Violin Concerto*, Movement II (mm. 1–4)

Example 1b *String Quartet No. 1* (mm. 1–3)

Example 1c *String Quartet No. 1* (Rehearsal No. 11, mm. 13–14)

Ferenc Bónis observes:

> We seem to recognize in the opening movement of the *String Quartet* the "slow motion film" of the quick concerto movement. The gay theme was transmuted into an expression of indescribable suffering. A prodigious chromatic tension, the precariousness of

the tonal "ground," the great rise and fall – all bear witness to the influence of Wagner's *Tristan und Isolde* even though without direct quotations from this music.[172]

Bartók characterizes the darkness of this transformation as his "Funeral Dirge."[173]

When Bartók quotes Stefi's leitmotif in his letters, it always stands for what he does not verbalize–his intimate feelings toward her. In his letter of November 29th, we find the musical outline of Stefi's motif asserting his love and solving it in hope–at least this is the meaning the music leads us to understand. "If you were here, then I could come to you at times, to 'regern', to argue and so on, and I would have even less time on rest and sleep."[174] He writes these words to her "just before the day broke,"[175] at the very moment when he spoke of having slept fewer than five hours. Bartók, however, did not wish to have written so bitterly, but he did so because of Stefi's coolness and intense indifference. And to say more, if there were even a token sign of her inclination toward Bartók, it would come as a divine revelation. He notes that if she were to put this cool unresponsiveness in writing, it would appear almost as her just being her natural self and his anticipating it, whereas her personal and verbal expression shows very little of it. And perhaps if he were asked, he would have to concede that being distant from her would likely be his preference–and that in order to keep his inspiration both safe and ideal. "I should not have written within this lugubrious sound–what is the use of writing motif image [Stefi's personification] in such a manner!"[176] We note here the seventh chord outline appears without the usual "D" resolution.

On the preceding evening Bartók stated that the main theme of the last movement was given birth together with its several variants, and he expressed his longing for her presence, although even here polarity and self-contradiction govern his mind. Her inspiration, though, remains strong and passionate:

> [Yesterday] I especially thought a lot about you; the main theme of the last movement of your concerto was born; also from this [second] movement this and that were derived. Although it is "better" for me that you are not here, I wished so much for you to be here. Could you tell me when you will come home, how many days before Christmas Eve, and

---

172 Ferenc Bónis, *Béla Bartók: His Life in Pictures and Documents* (Budapest: Corvina Press, 1981), 14. My study argues in favor of direct reference to Wagner's music drama.

173 Dille, "Angaben zum Violinkonzert 1907," 90–92. See also János Kárpáti, *Bartók's String Quartets*, 173.

174 Béla Bartók, *Briefe* (29 November 1907), no. 18, sec. 1.

175 Ibid.

176 Ibid.

then how long you will stay? I would harmonize it-in consonances!-just this once on your behalf.[177]

What follows is the musical excerpt of a jagged and angular descending motif along with Béla's description of it:

But you are rather close to that picture!...

The musical portrait of the ideal Stefi has been created-it is in existence-heavenly and intimate; as well as the one of impetuous Stefi Geyer is in existence-it is full of humor, witty, and it is brilliant. Now I have to create the portrait, that of indifferent, cool and aloof St. G. But it would be an awful music.[178] Oh no! I can see already lots of furrows on your forehead and your being angry. Okay, no more words like that; I am docking my feather quill. It is one hour past midnight again. All nine Muses should help you (if you at all need something like that).[179]

With respect to one side of the contrast, Bartók's letter of July 27th sent from Csíkkarcfalva quotes two musical excerpts from the nineteenth century. The main theme in the second movement of Beethoven's *String Quartet in C$^{\#}$ Minor*, Op. 131 (Movement II, mm. 1–4) evokes for him a "Grazioso" never more strongly felt. Beside it stands the world's sweeping grief motif of *Tristan*, and after that the composer's remark of gratitude toward Stefi: "I am very grateful to you for giving me a reason to offer these explanations, for they have left a mark on the question I was able to ask myself for the first time: what is the connection between the physical occurrence and, with that, the aroused feeling created by a chord like this one?"[180] Speaking of which, the grief of the "grave song" in Strauss's *Zarathustra* is weeping wretchedness rather than the more elusive shattering drama that comes with the opening measures of Wagner's opera.[181] Indeed, it is echoes of Strauss that we hear while listening to Stefi's *Concerto*, and Zarathustra's weeping in particular accounts somewhat for its texture.

---

177 Béla Bartók, *Briefe* (29 November 1907), no. 18, secs. 1 and 2.

178 Bartók depicted the "ugly image" of Stefi Geyer in the second of the *Two Portraits*, op. 5 ("A Caricature").

179 Béla Bartók, *Briefe*, no. 18, secs. 2–3.

180 Ibid., no. 4, sec. 14.

181 We might assume that this is a response to Stefi's concern, which is revealed to us in the letter of July 27th. It invites the controversial question: what is it in the particular presentation that induces an understanding of the musical expression-in what way is it reflected in music?

The anguished entry of the second subject (mm. 7–8) dramatizes the fate of Wagnerian "realism" and its great influence. Stefi's love motif and the grief motif of Tristan are fastened together here forever, and their motivic complementation is thus made clear. [**Ex. 2**] The last note, (A) of the subject, is the pivot to the second subject, which sets up the first polarization in the piece.

Example 2

The second subject (mm. 7–8) begins with F-E; together, this Subject 1/Subject 2 intersection (at A/FE) forms the first three notes of Wagner's opera.[182] This angular contour of the Subject 1/Subject 2 convergence (A/F-E-G-C#) foreshadows the jagged virtuoso theme of the second movement. [**Ex. 3**] Thus as mentioned earlier, the note A, as part of the A-F-E motif that elides Subject 1 and Subject 2 represents, the first implication of the fusion between the ideal and virtuoso–it is the spirit of *Tristan* that emerges as the catalyst.[183] Interestingly, Kárpáti explains a dual/polarized (love-death) meaning of the thematic transformation from its lively and dolce form in the *Concerto* to its darker appearance in the *Quartet*: "[the] yearning and resigned musical tone ... was inspired by [Bartók's] readings of Nietzsche and Schopenhauer.... Under such influences it was natural that the composer should express his passionate affection with the same musical character at his torment, resignation, and longing for death."[184]

Example 3

---

182 See n. 189. This chapter prominently identifies Tristan's grief and desire as fully expressed in the score.

183 The content of Chapter 6 provides more insight into the disruptive function of "F".

184 János Kárpáti, "Early String Quartets," *The Bartók Companion*, 226–227.

An even more dramatic polarization is seen between the solo violin (Stefi) and the string orchestra (Béla), which appropriates the two leitmotifs of Wagner's *Tristan* here. [**Ex. 4**]

Example 4 (Rehearsal No. 2)

These motifs are spelled out as clearly as possible to demonstrate the connection between music and the emotional meaning derived from it. The universal "love-leap" of minor/major sixths is presented in the duet between tutti and violin I, where one of the voices (Reh. No. 2, mm. 1–2) continues chromatically with the three-note motif (A-B♭-B) of Tristan's desire. Consequently, we find another polarization and see it perhaps as the primary one. Three leitmotifs with three different messages–love, grief, and longing–presented here in parallel treatment in the separate voices support our thesis that this is the precise moment in the *Concerto* in which Bartók attempts to make a fusion of opposites. This is an unparalleled moment in the work because polarity is essential to the whole conception of the *Concerto* and, indeed, to Bartók's entire life and thought. As Siegmund Levarie writes, such polarities are natural phenomena:

Polarity is an old and universal concept. Goethe called it one of the "great driving wheels of all nature" [*Naturwissenschaftliche Schriften* (Hamburg: Christian Wagner, 1955), p. 547]. Each of the following antithetical pairs forms a conceptual whole: day-night, male-female, inhaling-exhaling... God-Devil, good-bad–the phenomenalizations of polarity are endless. In music we may add up-down, loud-soft, fast-slow, wavelength-frequency, consonance-dissonance..... Polarity dominates the myths and religions of all ancient civilizations: China and India, Babylon and Egypt, Palestine and Greece. It provided the great Renaissance philosopher Nicolaus Cusanus with the central idea of *coincidentia oppositorum*, the coincidence of opposites as poles of a single unit reaches back to an old quoted Chinese text: "Music originates from measure and is rooted in the great One. The great One generates the two poles; the two poles generate the force of dark and light" [*Das Glasperlenspiel* (Frankfurt: Suhrkamp Verlag, 1966), p. 30].

Ideal polarity presupposes equal validity of the two complementary, opposing forces. Yet human prejudice often creates the paradox of our preferring one pole over the other. "Light day" seems to be a positive experience for most people, yet Schopenhauer and Tristan favored "dark night." Depending on one's nature, one clearly is attracted by one sex rather than the other. Is right better than left?[185]

The connecting principle in this passage is *chromatic compression and diatonic expansion,* which builds Bartók's passionate struggle and leads us to the authentic phenomena of the music. Also present here (Reh. No. 2, m. 5; tutti-violin II) is what one would call the first seeds of a new direction in Bartók's musical language: the octatonically-derived double-tritone tetrachord referred to later more simply as cell z (implied here in the three-note segment, $F^\#$-$C^\#$-C-[]).[186]

The G tonality of the fourth appearance of the love motif (Reh. No. 2, m. 5) is the symmetrical complement of the next entry on A (Reh. No. 4, m. 54) around the D-axis tonality.[187] Transformed into the key of G, the rising motif of Stefi

185 Siegmund Levarie, "Musical Polarity: Major and Minor," *International Journal of Musicology,* vol. 1 (1992), 29–30.

186 Leo Treitler first referred to this symmetrical tetrachord as cell z, in "Harmonic Procedure in the *Fourth String Quartet* of Béla Bartók," *Journal of Music Theory 3/2* (November, 1959), 292–297. Elliott Antokoletz has shown how this cell belongs to a larger system that is based on interval cycles and symmetrical pitch relations in Bartók's music, in "Principles of Pitch Organization in Bartók's Fourth String Quartet" (Ph.D. diss.) (New York: City University of New York, 1975).

187 See Béla Bartók's *Essays,* "Structure of Music for String Instruments," ed. Benjamin Suchoff (New York: St. Martin's Press, 1976), 416, in which he outlines this inversionally related succession of fugue entries of the slow movement. Thus the rigorous approach to such unfolding around an axis is already evident at this early date.

(G-B-D-F♯) does not stand by itself this time. Instead, the desire of Tristan changes its direction downwardly, polarizing the contour with the love melody. [**Ex. 5**] At this moment in the compositional development, it would be too early for the *Liebestod* since the solo violin seems to continue in the "life" implication of the rising-seventh chord.

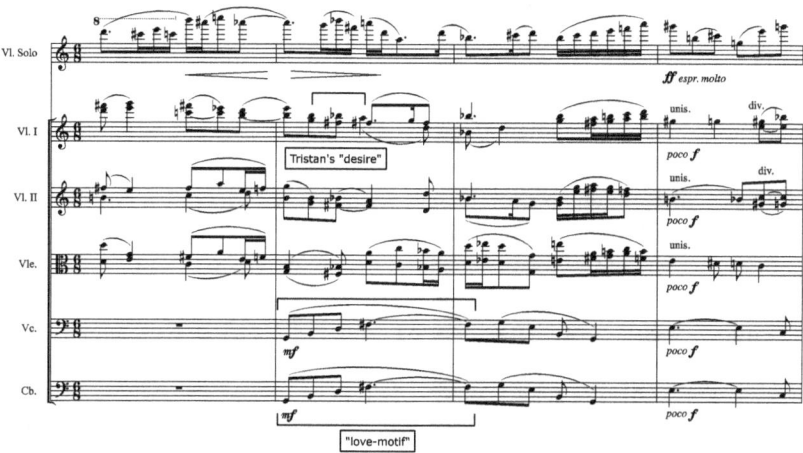

Example 5 (Rehearsal No. 2, mm. 5–6)

In the middle (more developmental) part of this movement, Bartók brings the last three notes of the motif of Tristan (A-B♭-B) into relation with a B-minor-seventh chord variation with added G♯ (B-D-F♯-[G♯]-A). [**Ex. 6**]

Example 6 (Rehearsal No.4)

Another elision occurs here, by means of a duplication of pitch-class B, between the Tristan segment and the latter form of the Stefi motif. The major sixth (B-G#) stands in conflict here with the grief motif that is initiated by the minor sixth. The integration of both motifs is achieved by one of the most identifiable techniques: a filling-in process or, more specifically, motivic pitch-set complementation.[188] Thus it seems that in the process of composing the work, Bartók must have arrived at the melodic and tonal design of the love motif by working out this combination a priori.[189] And one can now see the expanded symbolic meaning that comes across at that point of compositional momentum. The composer's trick is one of building the musical language on one basic melodic element throughout, combining and recombining it into different motifs according to his emotional state. The second motivic elision in this measure takes place between Tristan's longing–(or desire), []-A-Bb-B (Violin I), and the grief motif, the original form (A-F-E) being transposed here to F#-D-C# (viola). The chromatic segment of Tristan's longing (A-Bb-B) now forms a link by means of textural overlap between Stefi's transformed motif (B-D-F#-A) and Tristan's transposed grief motif (F#-D-C# (Reh. No. 4, mm. 8–9)).

It is striking that the Tristan chord is that of Stefi, that is, the specific F#-D-C# transposition of Tristan's grief motif (A-F-E), which contains three of the four notes of Stefi's opening seventh-chord.[190] Intrigue is deepened by placing the entire passage in the key of B (Reh. No. 4, mm. 8–12), which is heard as a diminution of the main fugue subject. The second subject answers twice as an isolated entry in the cor anglais and is made yet more prominent and autonomous by its repetition in the first oboe.[191] Although this represents an abbreviated statement of the main subject in contrast to the complete Subject 2 that is stated twice, it

---

188 In his *The Music of Béla Bartók* (Berkeley and Los Angeles: University of California press, 1984), Chapter 5, Antokoletz discusses the *Fifth String Quartet* in which the "filling-in" technique is entirely systematic. The *Concerto* already reveals this process.

189 In Béla's letter to Stefi of November 29th, we find the musical excerpt in which the D major-seventh chord is complemented by the Tristan chord; or, if we choose the dissolution within the ambiguity, the love-motif becomes twisted. It progresses from love to the darkness of death (the "funeral dirge" in the *First String Quartet*), but then opens again to the modal Hungarian world.

190 László Vikárius in *Modell és Inspiráció: Bartók zenei gondolkodásában* (Pécs: Jelenkor Kiadó, 1999), 96–97, regards Stefi's chord (D-F#-A-C#) as the result born out of the inspiration of the four-note chord that exists within the Tristan chord.

191 Here we encounter the same instrumentation that Wagner used for this motif.

is not a failure in Bartók's attempt to have established such a relation between them. Rather, it is a purposeful indication of Subject 2, representing Béla's taking over the focus from the Subject 1, which represents Stefi.

The end mirrors and clarifies the beginning. The closing statement of Bartók's musical autobiography is no longer hidden. That is to say, the retrograde form of Béla/Tristan's grief motif is unified with Stefi's love motif in the last measures of the *Andante sostenuto*. [**Ex. 7**]

Example 7 (Rehearsal No.8, mm. 8 to the end)

And yet it maintains its uniqueness as the "ideal" entity that we have known from the beginning. The same pivot note A (m. 7) serves as the point of departure (the penultimate measure before the end of the movement) for the two human beings to *rise above all*–toward the "ideal."

6 Form and Poetic Content

An inclusive interpretation of the *Concerto's* form, poetic content, and tonal/ harmonic language taken together serves to reveal the complex motivic and thematic strategies. The identity and transfigurations of the leitmotiv, both as determinants of style and process, are part of a larger system: a chain of thirds that functions as the underpinning for the leitmotivic succession throughout the work. The urgent presence of the *Tristan* grief motif (A-F-E) that is carried in the single voice of orchestra (violin 2 section only) joins Béla to Stefi at the cadential point of her first solo statement initiated with her motif–a manifesto of his love for and longing toward her. The presence of two of the greatest human emotions are revealed here in the first eight measures of the poetic work, which are then to be carried forward in order to project their meaning into the contrasting thematic ideas of the First and Second Movements. In this way the *Tristan* leitmotif takes on a secondary assignment by serving as bridge from the old to the new, the ideal to the real, and the octatonic romance of the cultured to the pentatonic modality of the peasant.

The order of movements in the *Concerto* was determined by the composer's emotional state toward the dedicatee of the composition. Four days before Christmas 1907, Béla wrote to Stefi that it was an absolute necessity that his concerto for her consist of two movements only–as the opposite sides of one portrait. Bartók wonders why the idea of making it a two-movement concerto came so late to him, and he admits that "a man opens his eyes rather seldom."[192]

This concept of two opposites–of a dynamic polarity–permeates the musical context and leads us into the transcendental message of the *Concerto*. A movement from diatonicism to pentatonicism by way of the chromatic state characterizes the opening statement of the first movement. [**Ex. 1**] This becomes the seed that generates the entire work. Structural and expressive levels are also determined by polarity. Diatonic expansion contrasting with chromatic compression[193] and smooth, arpeggiated contours contrasting with angular ones generate the two most significant moods of the *Concerto*. In addition, there are local juxtapositions. For instance, the polarity of dotted-versus-smooth rhythms serves to intensify

---

192 Béla Bartók, *Briefe an Stefi Geyer*, no. 21.
193 This is Bartók's own reference to a process which is basic to virtually all of his music. See *Béla Bartók Essays*, Suchoff, 381–383.

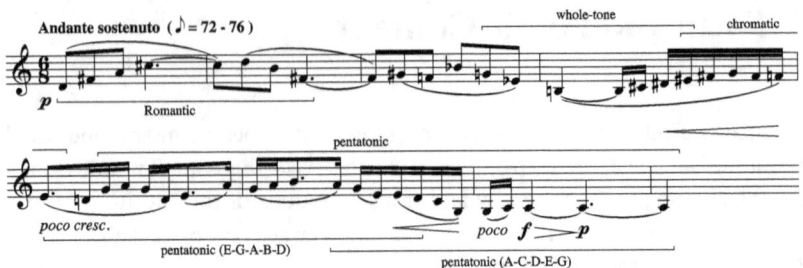

Example 1 (mm. 1–7)

Example 2 (mm. 7–8)

resolution, conflict, and ambiguity. This juxtaposition characterizes Hungarian folk music and pervades the textures throughout Bartók's works.[194]

Similar polarized concepts can be found in Bartók's thematic approaches as well. The thematic dimension turns the work into a coherent structure that is comprehensible on both purely musical and poetic levels. Thus the polarity between first and second subjects of the *Andante sostenuto* is most readily experienced. Linked by the first hint of the *Tristan* grief motif, A-F-E, **[Ex. 2]** this polarity governs the contrasting thematic ideas of first and second movements: soft, charming, and ideal, versus virtuoso, critical, and jagged. The fate of Wagnerian realism and its powerful influence are recorded in the desolate agony of the second subject (mm. 7–8). It is here that Stefi's love motif and Tristan's grief motif are forever wedded together, revealing their motivic complementarity. **[Ex. 2]** The final note

---

194 For instance, see the smooth beginning and dotted ending of the fugue subject in Bartók's *First String Quartet*, and the opening phrases of the *First Bagatelle*, op. 6. Furthermore, this rhythmic feature in Bartók's works can be traced to a fundamental syllabic pattern in the old Hungarian folk song style: 4/4 ♫♫♫ ♫♫♫ | ♪ ♩. ♩ ‖. See *Béla Bartók, The Hungarian Folk Song*, ed. Benjamin Suchoff (Albany: State University of New York, 1981), 32.

of the subject is A, serving as pivot to the second subject, which prepares for the *Concerto*'s first polarization. The grief motif then becomes the catalyst that takes us, in the spirit of *Tristan*, from one characterization to another.[195]

Although Stefi's motif is the primary structural component of the whole work, it is the elusive and only partially fulfilled *Tristan* reference that seals its joints and links its two poles: the diatonic and pentatonic spheres (measure 7 in **Example 2**). On a deeper level, this motif serves as a point of departure in the progression from the passionate major-seventh harmony of the "fin-de-siècle" world of Strauss to the pentatonic modality of the simple world of the peasant. The transition between the two is implemented by means of expansion from chromatic to whole-tone areas. By polarizing the pentatonic world of the Hungarian peasant, Bartók may be expressing his conviction that to escape the decadent urban society is to reconnect with peasant life. In this case, the drama evoked by the *Concerto* involves the symbolic interplay of three images: Stefi, Tristan, and the peasant.

Bartók is able to create his musical symbolism with a variation technique in which the smallest alteration of a motif can transform its meaning entirely. In some cases, motifs transform themselves gradually and logically, a technique he may have learned primarily from Beethoven, Brahms, or Wagner.[196] For instance, the second subject (F-E-G-C♯) may be seen as an intervallic mutation of the thematic segment G♯-F-Bb-G (mm. 3–4). These two measures already foreshadow the material of the new idea. The most significant presentation of Stefi's leitmotif appears at the first entry of woodwind instruments that carry the melody majestically at the unison and octave (see Chapter 5, **Example 4**). At the same time, the solo violin moves from the jagged octatonic-1 segment (Reh. No. 2, m. 2) to

---

195 On his way home on August 21, 1904 from Bayreuth to Regensburg, Bartók wrote to his friend, the Hungarian poet Kálmán Harsányi: "I am writing these lines under the effect of *Parsifal*. It is a very interesting work, but it did not have as tremendous an impact on me as *Tristan*" (Ferenc Bónis, "Bartók and Wagner" in *Bartók Studies*, ed. Todd Crow (Detroit: Information Coordinators, 1976), 86).

196 Bartók's early compositional education was founded prominently on Brahms, especially in the Pozsony years of the 1890s. He then studied the scores of Wagner extensively at the Royal Academy of Music (1899–1903), so the Wagnerian idiom began to manifest itself in his early masterworks. Bartók's own comment about the influence of Beethoven is well known in a reference to the formal impact on his music. With respect to the musical references to Beethoven in many of his works, compare, for example, the *Fifth String Quartet*'s finale with that of his Op. 131 in C♯. Also in Bartók's *First String Quartet*, the opening fugue was influenced by the opening slow fugue of Beethoven's Op. 131; see Kárpáti, 177.

the smoother, pentatonic one. The latter elides with the five-note whole-tone
segment (Reh. No. 2, m. 3), after which the broken intervallic gestures lead to the
next thematic design of Stefi's motif in the lower strings. This time, however, it is
on G (G-B-D-F$^{\#}$). The closer proximity of the leitmotifs creates the most intensified textural expression (see Chapter 5, **Example 5**).

What is the formal structure of both movements, and how does the thematic
material relate? The first movement, *Andante*, can be outlined as an ABA form.[197]
However, to categorize this movement simply as tripartite or perhaps rounded-
binary structure minimizes the significance of its textural process, namely that
of the fugue, the most obvious feature of which is the horizontal stratification
of thematic material. The specific design of the *Andante* is that of a two-subject
fugue in three sections. Its two subjects and their occurrences divide the movement into six structural units on different tonal plateaus. The fugal entries of
the first subject unfold in inversional fifth relations around the D tonic: D-A-
D-G (Reh. Nos. 1 and 2). This is followed in turn by a progression of tonalities
related by minor thirds, i.e. interval-3/9 cycle, D-F-A^{b}-B (Reh. Nos. 4 and 5). The
final thematic presentation begins with the first subject on A^{b}, which stands in
a tritone relation to the final entry on D. These two cyclic and intervallic tonal
schemes are essential to an understanding of the tension between one side of
the tonal polarity and the other: diatonicism and fifth relations as opposed to
octatonic and more chromatic minor-third relations. The two-subject fugue here
becomes the symbolic vehicle for the portrayal of two people: Stefi and Béla/
Tristan.

The outline of Movement I below shows both the large-scale and more local
significance of the two themes as first Subject (Stefi), second Subject (Béla/
Tristan), and their relations. It is the second subject, Tristan's grief, that is guided
by developmental strategies and called on to serve as the theme of the contrasting
subsidiary fugal exposition in the formal plan of the movement. [**Diagram 1**]

The first seven measures of the first subject form a symmetrical phrase closed
off by the Hungarian (short-long) rhythm. [**Example 1**] The opening phrase is
an ascending arpeggiated major-seventh chord, the most prominent motif of
the entire work. In the course of the movement this motif contracts from the
sonority of the traditional triadic idiom to the almost cellular function of the
chromatic Tristan transfiguration. The descending contour of the melodic idea

---

197 This large-scale formal design tabulates with Weiss-Aigner's formal interpretation;
     see Günter Weiss-Aigner, "The Lost Violin Concerto," in *The Bartók Companion*, ed.
     Malcolm Gillies (London: Faber and Faber, 1993), 468–476.

Diagram 1

MOVEMENT I: OUTLINE

(1) Introduction, Subject 1 and Subject 2 (16 measures)

D

(mm. 1–7)	(7–16)
Subject 1	Subject 2
Solo Violin	Tutti Violin I

(2) Subject 1, Fugal Exposition (24 measures)

D	A		D	G (transition)
(No. 1, mm. 1–7)	(No. 1, mm. 8–17)		(No. 2, mm.1–4)	(No. 2, mm. 5–7)
1st fugal entry	2nd fugal entry		3rd fugal entry	4th fugal entry
Tutti Vln I divisi	Tutti Vln I divisi, Vln II		Wind & Strings	Full Orchestra

(3) Interlude (17 measures)

F	A	F♯	D	B
(No. 3)	(No. 4, m. 1)	(No. 4, m. 2)	(No. 4, m. 3)	(No. 4, m. 5)
Solo "theme"	Solo Violin	"signaling"	leitmotifs	

(4) Subject 2, Fugal Exposition (14 measures)

Subject 2 (Clarinet)	Subject 2 (Oboe)	Subject 2 (String Stretto)
b	b	pitch entry A♭ C G♭ C [or B♭, D, A♭,D]
(No. 5)	(No. 5, m. 5)	(No. 5, mm. 8–14)

(5) Subject 1, Fugal Exposition (25 measures)

Subject 1

A♭	G	D
(No. 6)	(No. 7, m. 5)	(No. 8)

(6) Epilogue, Subject 1, Stefi's leitmotif (7 measures)

(No. 8, m. 8 to the end)

leitmotif

F♯	F♯	F♯	D
Solo Violin			

---

in measure 2 becomes the extension of Stefi's motif. Measures 3 and 4 foreshadow the material of Subject 2 (mm. 7–16)–a quasi-sequential idea in angular contour.

What distinguishes the second subject from the first subject is its intervallic compression. While both subjects are analogous in thematic contour, their intervallic structure is different. The original thematic segment (m. 3) has a boundary of a perfect fourth (F-B♭) in G♯-F-B♭-G, the second subject a boundary of a tritone (G-C♯) in F-E-G-C♯. The perfect fourth creates a diatonic sense, which is borne out by the larger four-note segment itself (F-G-G♯-B♭; in enharmonic spelling, F-G-A♭-B♭). In the second subject, the tritone indicates octatonicism, which is confirmed by the larger four-note segment, C♯-E-F-G (mm. 7–8). It is the difference in intervallic structure and the similarity of melodic contour between these two themes that create both their polarity and their unity.

At the point of suggested anticipation of the second subject (m. 3), there is a change in the density of sound and the linear shape of the first phrase. The subject moves from the smooth, diatonic motif into the more narrow, jagged elements of the chromatic segment. The diatonic implication of the four-note segment, B♭-G-E♭-B (m. 3), is part of the larger linear segment that outlines a more chromatic continuum. If we transform this segment (m. 3) chromatically and place it into the opening D major-seventh configuration, then all of the notes beginning with pitch-class B (m. 2) and ending with pitch-class B (m. 4) are new, E♭-F-[F♯]-G-G♯-B♭-B, except for the F♯ which repeats the third degree of the former. Thus we also sense a kind of polymodal chromaticism resulting from the emergence (in m. 3) of the prominent diatonic segment G♯-F-B♭-G-E♭ (in enharmonic spelling and diatonic scale ordering E♭-F-G-A♭-B♭). The melodic contour of this segment foreshadows the second subject. This diatonic segment (E♭-F-G-G♯-B♭) utilizes almost all of the remaining notes outside the D-major-seventh chord. In other words, the initial main element of the subject (D-F♯-A-C♯) and the ensuing configuration (G♯-F-B♭-G-E♭) that foreshadows the second subject, both of which are diatonic, complement each other in two ways: by mutual exclusivity in the pitch content, and by a smooth contour instead of a jagged one. The resulting chromaticism points the direction of the work toward a smaller, dissonant, and "painful" element.[198]

The close-knit, continuous fabric in which these basic elements are integrated creates ambiguity from the very beginning.[199] And the arch shape of the

---

198 This interpretation is supported by other Bartók works of this period stemming from the time of the *Concerto* up to *Duke Bluebeard's Castle*.

199 A similar process characterizes the *First String Quartet*.

theme provides a sense of structure by its two perfectly balanced phrases. In the subject itself, the first phrase (mm. 1–4) moves up and the second (mm. 4–7) down, with the two halves together rounding out the structure. As part of this arch shape, the diatonic material of the leitmotif is compressed into a whole tone and then into a chromatic segment within an increasingly active rhythm. The pentatonic portion (m. 5) injects a peasant world reference into the polarized–yet first-subject derived–second subject. As a manifestation of the diatonic-chromatic relations, this shape is projected into the large-scale arch shape of the movement.

The *Allegro giocoso*–Movement II and the *Concerto's* finale, [**Diagram 2**]–differs from the first movement in its multiple sections of contrasting characters. Here Stefi's leitmotif (D-F#-A-C#) takes on a virtuoso identity. Its disjunctive appearance portrays perhaps the more realistic and caustic side of the young woman's personality. The opening theme, played by the solo violin, forms a musical sentence of three contrasting phrases–phrase a (mm. 1–4), phrase b (mm. 5–6), and phrase c (mm. 7–8)–that reflects the contrasts of the opening phrase (mm. 1–4). [**Diagram 2**] The first five-note motif (D#-F#-A#-C-E), with its harmonic component of the augmented-sixth chord (C-E-F#-A#), represents a sonority within a partially octatonic collection. In contrast to the conjunct legato theme of the first movement, the theme of the second movement (mm. 1–13) offers a downward motion that is finally countered by the rhythmic action of the upward-oriented closing phrase. This is itself countered, however, by the downward motion of the melodic line played by flute and clarinet.

Although the opening theme of the second movement has a different extrinsic character from that of the first movement, both themes relate to each other intrinsically. If we align their five notes respectively, we find that the differences of pitch correspondence (D#-versus D, A# versus A, C versus C#) produce an out-of-focus distortion of Stefi's leitmotif. This difference plays a prominent role in the global picture of the leitmotif's transformation in the *Concerto* and beyond. [**Fig. 1**] The first phrase moves in the direction of the C-major chord in its root position and then its dominant, G. There are four measures of the opening theme where the melodic line is descending and the rhythmic pattern forms an arch shape. The theme begins with an even, almost march-like, pulse that changes to a faster dotted rhythm. The arrival point is the whole-note (G). The entire score at this point is divided into two textural levels.

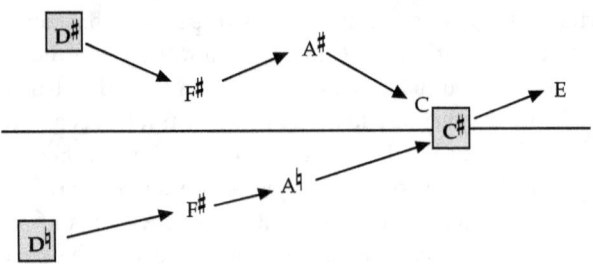

Figure 1 (Illustration of Stefi's leitmotifs I and II)

The formal structure of the second movement can be viewed either in the form of ritornello/rondo, sonata-allegro, or both. **[Diagrams 2 and 3]** It is a mistake to force the movement into an abstract scheme of either one of the traditional forms.[200] Weiss-Aigner, who places the movement in the Sonata-Allegro form, concedes this fallacy:

> Ever since Bartók's first symphonic attempt in 1902 a tendency is discernible in his compositions overlaying traditional sonata form with several transitional thematic sections. That tendency assumed a more definite form in this second movement. Of course, the two passages of development of the subsidiary theme and of the third theme can be interpreted entirely within the return relationship expected between exposition and recapitulation, just as the entry of the main theme at No. 25 (linked contrapuntally with the third theme) can be taken as the beginning of the recapitulation. But the many "development sections" which begin afresh from the initial motif of the movement can only be accommodated within this sonata-form framework with considerable difficulty.[201]

Diagram 2 (Musical Example follows [**Ex. 3**])

MOVEMENT II: RITORNELLO/RONDO FORM
A Ritornello/Rondo Refrain (13 measures). [**Ex. 3**] Solo and tutti ending with a solo cadenza.

A						
m			m^1			n
a	b	c	a1/d	a1/d	c/e	Solo cadenza
1m.	1m.	2mm.	1m.	1m.	2mm.	
4		+	4		+	5

---

200 Bartók's use of overlapping or intersecting formal concepts is typical of the multi-dimensional structural of his thought and can be related to his conception of "variants" in his folk music research.

201 Weiss-Aigner, 474–475.

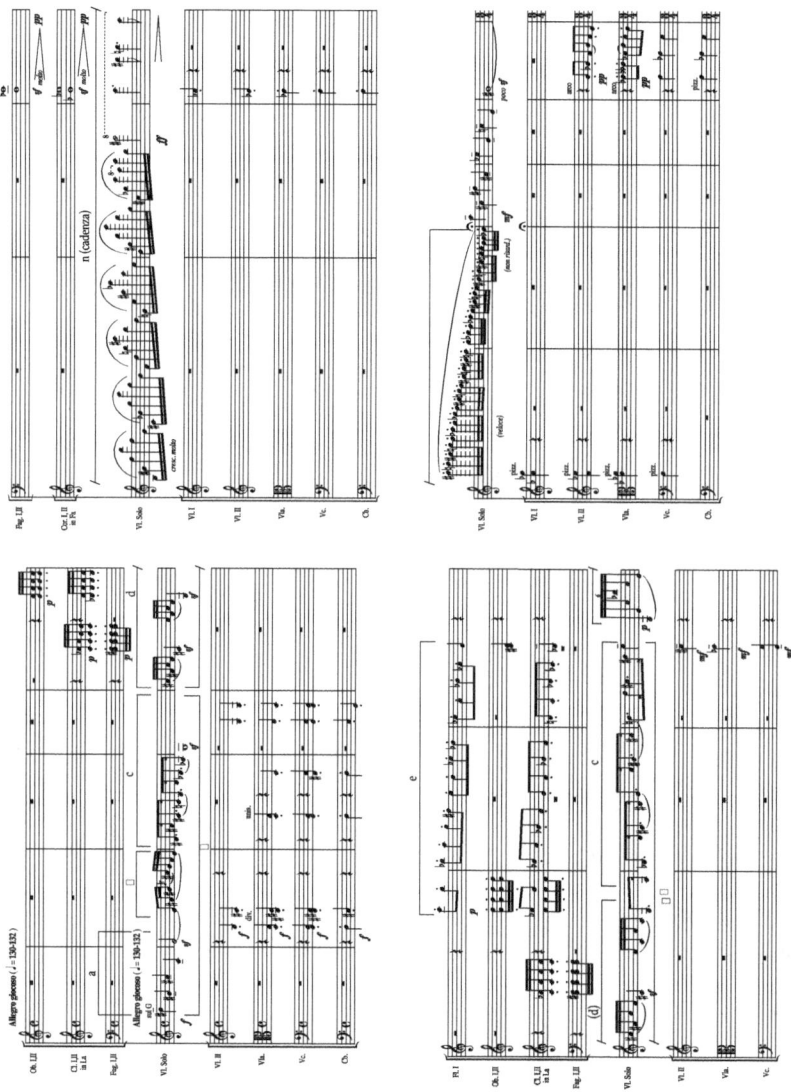

Example 3 (Ritornello/Rondo Refrain A)

Diagram 3

MOVEMENT II: FORMAL OVERLAYS

Sonata Form		Ritornello/Rondo Form
Exposition (107 mm.)		*Ritornello 1*
Theme 1		*Rondo Refrain:* A
A		A
A^1	m. 14	A^1
A^2	Reh. no. 12	A^2
Theme 2		*Episode 1:* B
B	Reh. no. 12, m. 11	B
Theme 3		
C	Reh. no. 14, m. 5	C
Development	(87 mm.)	*Ritornello 2*
Theme 1		*Rondo Refrain:* A
A^3	Reh. no. 16, m. 15	A^3
A^4	Reh. no. 17, m. 9	A^4
Motivic transformations		*Episode 2* (developmental): C
D	Reh. no. 17, m. 20	D
E	Reh. no. 19, m. 10	E
F	Reh. no. 23	F
Recapitulation (58 measures)		*Ritornello 3*
Theme 1		*Rondo Refrain:* A
A^5	Reh. no. 24	A^5
A^6/C	Reh. no. 25	A^6/C
Theme 2		*Episode 3:* B
B	Reh. no. 28	B
Theme 3		
C	Reh. no. 30	C
Quote:		Quote:
Der Esel ist ein Dummes Tier		*Der Esel ist ein Dummes Tier*
G	Reh. no. 30, m. 7	G
Coda (39 measures)		*Ritornello 4*
Theme 1		*Rondo Refrain:* A
A^7	Reh. no. 31	A^7
Theme 3		Coda
C	Reh. no. 31, m. 8	C
Cadenza		*Cadenza*
Quote:		Quote:
Stefi's leitmotif from Mvt. I		Stefi's leitmotif from Mvt. I
Closing Tutti		Closing Tutti
D	Reh. no. 34, m. 4	D

The diagram of Movement II shows five independent themes (B, C, D, E, F) in addition to the opening A (Ritornello). **[Diagram 3]** The first three themes are recapitulated according to the sonata-allegro conception; the last two (E and F) appear only once. As discussed earlier in this Chapter and Chapter 5, Bartók also identified theme B as Stefi's leitmotif. He drew attention to this theme not only in his letter to Stefi (October 1907), but also in the *Concerto* itself by working with it on five pages of the orchestral score. The theme first appears at what is almost the midpoint of the *Concerto* (m. 171 of 354 measures, Theme B). Its tempo and metric change–*Meno allegro e rubato* ($\downarrow$= 100) in C time–create the first impression of bearing a quasi-slow movement. What comes to mind at this point is Carl Dahlhaus' comment on Liszt's "relativized" formal categories: "At times it is virtually impossible to tell whether a passage is a second theme or a slow movement."[202] The theme seems magnified in its proportion within the local position or even in its relation to the whole movement. If someone were missing the slow movement in our *Concerto*, it would be tempting to look at this particular theme as the place to find it.

According to Weiss-Aigner, the next independent musical idea, Theme C, represents "a third Straussian theme, [which] draw[s] its inspiration from bar 2 of the opening theme."[203] It acquires a function of a transitional thematic unit. However, against this Straussian assumption, one may argue that the unusual form of the *Concerto* appears to have roots in the lassu and friss of the verbunkos style. The quality of slow, free tempo in an otherwise Wagnerian idiom points to the parlando-rubato style of lassu. In addition to this form, there are motivic sixteenth-note passages that are quasi-ostinato and which accelerate at certain points in the second movement. Yet Theme C actually has the quality of an incessant sixteenth-note pattern of the verbunkos style.

Theme D is a rhythmic and physical gesture. It is a folk-like quaternary structure, ABAC, which is very different from the Wagnerian longing evoked by the linearly continuous expression of the opening cumulative movement. Theme D is the one that confirms the work's folk-like quality. With its mixture of Hungarian and Slovak folk elements, the structure is clear and balanced, with the tempo giusto dance-like quality contributing to its classical character. And yet the music is not purely in the old Hungarian folk song style because

---

202 Carl Dahlhaus, *Nineteenth-Century Music* (Berkeley and Los Angeles: University of California Press, 1989), Eng. trans. James Bradford Robinson, 239.
203 Ibid., 472.

its stanzaic structure is not isometric. In his 1924 book, *A Magyar Népdal*,[204] Bartók describes the folk melodies and gives the most characteristic examples. There are many different patterns that characterize the tempo giusto rhythm. In Bartók's Class C (the classification of folk sources), this is a mixture of both old Hungarian folk song and foreign (Slovak) elements, with heterometric or isometric strophes. According to this classification, Theme D would fall into this category since it contains non-corresponding elements that are not purely of the old or new style. Rather, it exhibits the heterogeneous elements of both old Hungarian and Slovak folk song characteristics. This combination suggests that the theme is characteristic of Bartók's Class C mixed style because it does not exhibit any unity of style.[205] When peasants went to the cities, they came in contact with the modern, popular Hungarian tunes of the time. By assimilating these characteristics, they created a new style of Hungarian folk music which nevertheless retained its purely Hungarian and homogeneous genius. However, when Hungarian peasants in the cities also heard tunes of the Slovak- and Romanian-speaking peoples living within the greater Hungarian territory, they adopted them too, and converted them into the Hungarian mixed style.

Theme E represents a laughing character–perhaps more a cry than a laugh. While Wagner's scream is significantly marked in *Parsifal* and *Götterdämmerung*, the cry manifestation of Béla/Tristan is expressed as an emotional release. Hence the issue in the *Concerto* is perhaps more one of physical pain than that of pure emotion. Theme F is actually Theme A as manifesting the jagged melodic contour within a "Caffe Haus" triviality.

What we have labeled Theme G in our analytical outline is not an original tune but a quotation of the popular song "Der Esel ist ein Dummes Tier" ("The Donkey is a Foolish Beast"). Preceded by the varied recapitulation of Themes B and C, and followed by a return of Theme A, it is an unexpected and startling intrusion into the movement. How can one interpret its presence? Weiss-Aigner maintains that it "simply reflects the composer's memory of happy hours spent singing in the company of the violinist [Stefi] and her brother."[206] A purely musical explanation might suggest that it provides the type of emotional relief that we find in many later works of Bartók as well–the light and popular, however, functioning amidst the more serious and dense surroundings as an element

---

204 See Béla Bartók, *The Hungarian Folk Song*, Suchoff, 1–80.

205 Ibid., ex. no. 121, p. 252 from 1906 [I. Keszthely (Zala)].

206 Weiss-Aigner, 475.

of relief at the breaking point.[207] The greater the tension, the greater the need for a simple idea to break that tension, and that is the structural as well as expressive function of such a tune. The aesthetic situation parallels Bartók's personal situation with Stefi at that time with the reappearance of Theme A.

To conclude, we entertain a thought about how the final ritornello or a sonata-like coda articulates a magnificent ending for the *Concerto*. The last 39 measures (Reh. No. 31) mirror and magnify both the musical essence and the poetic meaning of the whole work. At the point of the soloist cadenza (Reh. No. 33), nine measures of *Poco più agitato* placed before the tempo changes from *Allegro giocoso* to *Lento* (Reh. No. 34), Bartók brings back Stefi's leitmotifs successively and simultaneously, and with them, a high degree of compositional unity. The arrival of the C-major-seventh-chord domain is indeed a glorious moment in both Bartók's *Concerto* and his musical autobiography. The gradual transformation of the powerful leitmotivic idea is here fulfilled.

---

207 The following are examples to support such musical solutions: the basic bitonal A/Bb major tune at No. 769 of the Fifth Movement of the *Fifth String Quartet, Concerto for Orchestra* (an "Interroto" theme that parodies the Shostakovich *Seventh Symphony*), and the Burletta from the *Sixth Quartet*.

7 Stefi's Leitmotif: Variants and Transformations

As we have argued, Stefi's leitmotif becomes a personal and passionate voice in the life and work of the young composer. Bartók's music and letters begin by reminding us of how he began. In the *Concerto*, the composer, with the echo of the footsteps of past memory, presents us with the present and leads us into the future. The leitmotif is much more than a call signaling for us to be reminded of what transpired. It becomes a life-shaping presence that makes its way forward by looking back and retrieving what was lost in new forms. It gives grounds for desire, passion, and trust. And in the end it leaves us with a stream of hope. To appreciate the temporal character of the work, we must submit ourselves to the transfigurations of the leitmotif, the transformations they in turn generate, and through the work, in the hearer. The presence of leitmotifs is also essential to the compositional process of the *Concerto*, as suggested by Bartók's calling the opening motif of the first movement a "leitmotif." [**Ex. 1**]

Andante sostenuto (♪ = 72-76)

Example 1 (m. 1)

That he identified this leitmotif with Stefi Geyer gives it extra-musical significance on a personal and intimately private level.[208] In the tradition of Wagner and Strauss, the leitmotif is not simply a signaling device but creates, pervades, and interprets the environmental texture. Changing the moods throughout the *Concerto* are generated and expressed by the degrees of clarity or ambiguity evoked by the leitmotif's variants and transformations. We might even propose that whatever shape the leitmotif assumes at any particular moment is both cause and effect of the most prominent structural points in the score.

The progression of the entrances of Stefi's leitmotif as fugue subject proceeds by perfect fifths, a fourth, or a tritone: D-A-D-G-A♭-G-D. In the interludes (Reh.

---

208 *Béla Bartók Letters*, Demény, 43.

No. 3), the thematic contour embellishes the major and minor thirds of the original leitmotif in descending order of the F-major triad. The first and last thematic statements enter on F and B, with filling-in statements of the seventh chord on A, F#, and D. The tonal movement of the whole fugue is outlined in the following key progression: D-A-D-G-[F-A-F#-D-B]-Ab-G-D. Within this chain of key relations, the leitmotifs express different moods. This permits us to identify the tonal points and their function as landmarks on a continuous roadway of motivic development and probe the relation between the motivic variants and transformations.

We first turn to the underlying theoretical principle–diatonic expansion and chromatic compression–that governs the entire compositional aesthetic of Bartók. His own words support this primary conception that accounts for all of the transformations of the leitmotif.[209] The relation between both variants and transformations of the leitmotif falls within this aesthetic principle and may be subsumed under two levels in the compositional process: (1) the migration of the main subject from the Romantic ideal world to the Hungarian peasant world by way of the compressed range at the midpoint of the opening theme, and (2) the concept of contraction and expansion as the point of departure for understanding the transformative process within the developmental thread of the leitmotif. This process within the subject contains in microcosm the entire system for the progression of the leitmotivic variants, the foundation of which is a descending chain of thirds. On a deeper level, this motion of thirds comprehends the developmental thread of the leitmotif. In the system of third transpositions, two basic forms of the leitmotif are embedded: the major-seventh chord of Romantic harmony (M3-m3-M3), and the minor-seventh chord of pentatonic peasant modality (m3-M3-m3). Bartók himself tells us that it was precisely in 1907, the year of the *Concerto*, that he discovered pentatony in Hungarian folk music during his research in the Csík district.[210]

The significance of leitmotivic transformation is reflected on the microscopic level of the fugue subject in the transpositional shift to a new surface identity (C-E-G-B) of the same major-seventh chord (D-F#-A-C#). In the process of

---

209 Béla Bartók *Essays*, ed. Suchoff, 381.

210 *Béla Bartók, The Hungarian Folk Song*, Suchoff, 17–18. Antokoletz discusses new principles and their origins in the compositional language of Bartók: "Of these origins two extremes are seen in the ultra-chromaticism of German late Romantic music, on the one hand, and the pentatonic-diatonic modality of peasant music, on the other" (*The Music of Béla Bartók* (Berkeley and Los Angeles, University of California Press, 1984)), 312.

metamorphosis by means of the tunnel–the moment of total chromatic compression–Bartók himself undergoes metamorphosis through filtration autobiographically. And from this process the "pure gold" of C-major emerges, that is, the final purification of the D major-seventh chord. At the same time, the octatonic, whole tone, and chromatic textures within the theme acquire a catalytic function. The material is filtered, but the essence is retained.

Although the thematic surface changes by means of interval expansion and compression, the identity of Stefi's leitmotif is projected into every moment of the composition. The microcosmic continuum of leitmotivic manifestation based on intervallic contraction marks the path for the macrocosmic unfolding of the opening thematic content. This projection of the motivic essence into the larger structure points to those moments in the *Concerto* where essential variants occur and character transformations emerge. These changes are embodied in both the metamorphosis as well as the identity of thematic content and articulated tonalities.

The process of thematic transfiguration relies entirely on the contraction of the intervallic structure of the basic major-seventh chord. This contracting intervallic structure of this chord is paralleled by the direction of the tonal scheme. All of the entries of the main subject in the fugal exposition of the *Andante* unfold in perfect fifths, the primary interval of Stefi's motif: D-A and F#-C# represent one of the three interval-couples (D-A/F#-C#, D-F#/A-C# and the nonequivalent axial dyads D-C#/F#-A) of the major-seventh chord, D-F#-A-C#. Each of these fugal entries represents a different tonal level: D (Reh. No. 1), A (Reh. No. 1, m. 8), D (Reh. No. 2), and G (Reh. No. 2, m. 5). While these are only fifth and fourth entries, their association with the motif has a deep-level significance. As the intervals of the leitmotif contract from the major-modal tertian construction (especially from the fifths, D-A and F#-C#) to the most radically contracted stage at x-cell (mm. 3–4), so will the fugal fifth entries contract to a smaller intervallic stage: the perfect fourth (D-G) and the tritone (D-A♭). The fifth-transposing statements of the motif are built on these fifths: A-D-G (A-C#-E-G#, D-F#-A-C#, and G-B-D-F#). They consequently form the following superstructure in descending order: G#-E-C#-A̲-F#-D̲-B-G̲. The octatonic language, which in the micro-projection comprises alternating whole-and half-steps, is made up of interlocking tritones, whereas the diatonic chain, based on tertian structure, has interlocking fifths. The subsequent replacement of the fifth entries by tritone has octatonic (chromatic) significance.

The first interlude emerges as a disruption of the tonal situation of the fugue exposition. Following the basic shape of the leitmotif in the bass on G (Reh. No. 2, m. 5), a major-ninth chord, F-A-C-[]-G, introduces the F major area. [**Ex. 2**] The melodic theme played by the solo violin (F-C-A-F-D-B♭-G-F) can be viewed as Stefi's leitmotif hidden within this F-major configuration unfolding in gaps. Its descending contour anticipates a series of leitmotivic phrases progressing in thirds.

Example 2 (Rehearsal No.3)

A sequence of the leitmotif–on A as major-seventh chord (A-C#-E-G#), on F# as minor-seventh chord (F#-A-C#-E#), and on D as augmented-seventh chord (D-F#-A#-C#)–shows Bartók approaching a new whole tone partitioning by way of major thirds rather than whole tone per se in this transitional compositional momentum. [**Ex. 3**]

Example 3 (Rehearsal No. 4, mm. 1–3)

In other words, he avoids radical and abrupt change by using the major third, a property of Stefi's ideal. He then transforms it into a succession: M3-m3-M3, m3-M3-M3, M3-M3-m3. The roots of these clearly manifested seventh chords (A, F♯, and D) then become the components of the next seventh chord–on B (B-D-F♯-[G♯]A)–in the succession of leitmotivic transformation where a passing note is added to transform the Romantic mood into the whole tone countenance of the leitmotif.

There is another aspect that is telescoped in parallel fashion to the context of the fugal interludes: the Tristan reference already encountered. The significance of the F major area is one of "expressive doubling." Lawrence Kramer defines this term as a form of repetition, but a polarity of opposites as well:

> alternative versions of the same pattern define a cardinal difference in perspective.... The practice of expressive doubling is closely bound up with the utopian esthetics and subject/object polarity of early Romantic culture. As illocution, doubling gives the utopian project of art a concrete lyric or dramatic shape. It inscribes the sought for historical progress from the actual to the ideal within a definite temporal frame: the unfolding rhythm of the individual work or the developmental interval between two works.
> It follows that the terms of an expressive doubling form a hierarchy; one term represents a freer, happier, or more enlightened condition than the other. Or, to be more exact, one term represents the transposition of the other to a higher or deeper plane, a more brilliant or profound register.[211]

F's disruptive function here was anticipated at the juncture of the leitmotif and the second subject (m. 9). At this point, A-F-E represents the culmination of the descending sequence of "Stefi-Bartók," where it earlier had served as personification of Béla-Tristan. In this momentum of tonal disruption, the vertical ninth chord projects two of these notes (F and A) of that grief statement. Hence the eternal "love-leap" of the minor sixth (A-F) is now projected as the major third (F-A). While the intervallic reference of the major third (F-A) is retained in its long-range transpositional reflection of the basic D-F♯, its pitch-level significance now alters the major-third property to minor.

As already significantly encountered, the desire motif (A-B♭-B) of Tristan occurs in counterpoint to the G major-seventh chord–G-B-D-F♯–and the D major-seventh chord, D-F♯-A-C♯ (Reh. No. 2, m. 5). The Tristan segment is not only a temporal link between the D and G seventh chords (that is, it occurs simultaneously with both), but also an intervallic link in the process of contraction.

---

211 Lawrence Kramer, *Music as Cultural Practice, 1800–1900* (Berkeley and Los Angeles: University of California Press, 1990), 22, 30.

Each transposition of Stefi's leitmotif (major-seventh chord), which represents the larger diatonic intervallic stage, is contrapuntally juxtaposed with the Tristan segment. This represents the opposite extreme of chromatic compression from the major seventh chord to the x-cell tunnel. In these two occurrences, the process is simultaneous. In other words, both intervallic extremes–diatonic major-seventh chord and chromatic x-cell construction (incomplete), []-A-B♭-B–are identified in a unified relation.

The connection between the two extremes is actually an identity since the relation is based on a specific filling-in process. [**Fig. 2**] In the case of D-F♯-A-C♯, the Tristan A-B♭-B segment fills in the upper third (A-C♯) chromatically–D-F♯-A-[AB♭B]-C♯–with a whole-step gap between the last notes (B and C♯). In the case of G-B-D-F♯ (Reh. No. 2, m. 5), the Tristan A-B♭-B segment fills in the lower third (G-B) chromatically–G-[AB♭B]-B-D-F♯–with a whole-step gap between the lowest two notes (G-A). This large-scale process of inversional filling (D-F♯-[A-B♭-B]-C♯ and G-[A-B♭-B]-D-F♯) implies the presence of the central unfilled seventh chord (B-D-F♯-A) on B:

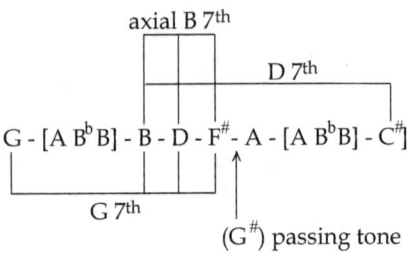

Figure 2

The latter appears, then, explicitly at Reh. No. 4, m. 5. Analogous to the simultaneously placed whole-steps (G-A and B-C♯) in the chromatically modified D and G seventh forms, the axial B minor-seventh chord (B-D-F♯-A) also incorporates within itself whole tone intrusions (B-[D-[]-F♯-[]]-A). This anticipates the whole tone area, with the added passing note G♯ in the upper third (F♯-A) being drawn into that sphere.

The next interlude stage in the sequence of signal-like occurrences of the main leitmotif is the B seventh-chord transposition in the strings. [**Ex. 4**] This special intermediary form, B-D-F♯-[G♯]-A, which the context will bear out as a hybrid combination of elements from the latter two forms[212]–ideal and pentatonic (see **Figure 2**)–contains a passing note (G#). This is a raised sixth that allows a whole tone detail to emerge, which is so essential to the sense of mood transformation.[213] Hence the pentatonic modality becomes an important link between the Straussian harmony and whole tone (D-F#-G#). Part of the transcendent quality of this hybrid form is in its tendency toward the funereal form (m3-M3-M3), where the lower third is contracted to minor. The funereal form, as we shall see later, indeed contains the elements for whole tone transformation. The minor-seventh chord, B-D-F#-A, represents a stage of compression stemming from the larger intervals of the original major-seventh chord, D-F#-A-C# (Stefi's love motif).

Example 4 (Rehearsal No. 4, m. 5)

There are certain possibilities between these two primary forms that belong to the chain of thirds. For instance, B-D-F#-A (m3-M3-m3) is the link between the ideal, which alternates within the chain, and the form that Bartók referred to as his "funeral dirge," F-Ab-C-E in connection with the *First String Quartet*.[214] The latter (m3-M3-M3) stands outside of the diatonic chain of thirds and leads us into the whole tone world because of its two adjacent major thirds. It is surprising if not shocking to confront this variant of Stefi's leitmotif in the score of the *Concerto*. Inverted in the intervallic structure, this seventh chord appears in the third and fourth measures of the opening fugue subject and, with its "funereal" meaning, stands between the ideal of Stefi and that of the peasant. [**Ex. 5**] We might wonder if the descending contour of this funereal hint is there to bring Stefi's major-seventh chord into Tristan's catalyst before rising again into the pure

---

212 It is hybrid because it combines the major third (D-F#) of the major-seventh form of Stefi's ideal with the minor thirds (B-D and F#-A) of the pentatonic minor seventh chord of the Hungarian peasant.

213 As Antokoletz has shown, the whole tone pitch collection serves as a chosen vehicle for the fatalistic realm expressed in *Bluebeard's Castle* in contrary to the diatonic material that corresponds with the human realm ("Bartók's *Bluebeard*: The Sources of Its Modernism," *College Music Symposium* 30/1 (Spring 1990), 75–95)).

214 Denijs Dille, "Angaben zum Violinkonzert, 1907," 90–92.

world of Hungarian peasants.[215] Is it possible that all of these feelings so different in their meaning and always apart from each other were present from the very beginning, and were then carried into the composition in a single line of the solo violin statement?

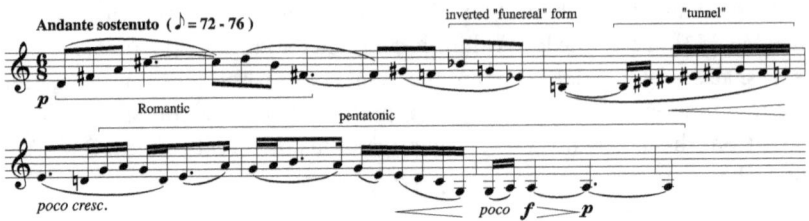

Example 5 (opening statement, mm, 1–7)

In the succession of fugal entries, the principle of contraction is evident. The fugal entry into the fugue recapitulation (Reh. No. 6) gives us tritone associations in place of fifths: D/A♭. The next entry (Reh. No. 7, m. 5) returns to the G tonality, which was encountered in the fugue exposition already as the basis of an incomplete subject statement. Taking the latter into account in the succession of entries, a new chromatic contrapuntal segment replaces the Tristan x-cell. In contrary motion with the ascending G major-seventh chord in the lower strings, the solo violin unfolds the complete symmetrical tetrachord of two tritones a half-step apart, referred to earlier as z-cell (G-F#-C#-C).[216] [**Fig. 3**] The significance of the z-cell replacing the x-cell is twofold: (1) the z-cell as a combination of two half-steps separated by a perfect fourth (G-F#-C#-C), which represents an expansion of the x-cell axis (half-step); and (2) one of the two axes of this z-cell (G-C-C#-F#) now mapping symmetrically into the G major-seventh chord literally, as shown:

---

215 It is the same descending seventh construction (m3-M3-M3) that gives the first entry (M3-M3-m3) for Judith in Bartók's 1911 opera, *Bluebeard's Castle*, Rehearsal No. 3, m. 2. See this parallel in Elliott Antokoletz, *Musical Symbolism in the Operas of Debussy and Bartók* (New York and Oxford: Oxford University Press, 2004).

216 See Chapter 5, n. 186.

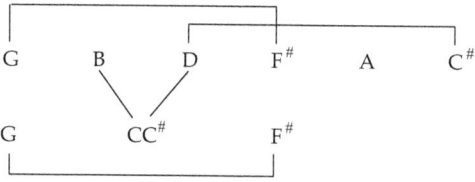

Figure 3

The importance of point (1) is that a re-expansion from chromatic x-cell to the more diatonic z-cell prepares for the return to the primary D major-seventh chord transposition (Reh. No. 8) in order to reinforce the arch form. This imputes a large-scale significance to the x-cell tunnel of the fugue subject, where the x-cell has served as intermediary between the D major-seventh chord and the break-through into the pentatonic and diatonic spheres of the embedded C major-seventh chord. The significance of point (2) is the Tristan x-cell ([]-A-B♭-B) that fills in upper and lower thirds of the D and G major-seventh chords to produce a larger segment around the B minor-seventh chord axis (B-D-F#-A). The z-cell now fills in the local axis of symmetry of the G major-seventh chord. Thus the move toward chromatic compression is implemented by an encirclement of the ideal motif with its extreme transformation–compressed identity, i.e., x-cell. A further goal is to complete the encircling process by approaching the center of the ideal directly and combining the G major-seventh chord with its symmetrical complement: [**Fig. 4**]

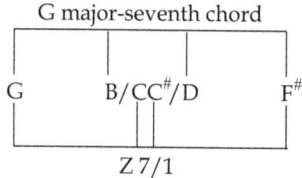

Figure 4

Thus the relation between the two extremes (diatonic and chromatic) is drawn together in this systematic process to reveal the identity of the ideal with the tunnel. These two polarized yet identical leitmotivic phrases are merely the extremes for an otherwise coherently related succession of leitmotif variants.[217] Whereas the context of the whole tone-distorted variants signifies and confirms this identity by appearing within its proper place in the process as in the fugue subject on the large-scale level, it occurs most significantly at Stefi's third leit-motif of Movement II. Tristan's motif as a catalyst once again is not a final stage in this process but serves a purpose in the whole compositional continuum. Increasingly in our discussion, this process of expansion and contraction will bring an explication of the fundamental principle governing the entire composi-tion. The final statement of the love motif appears at the closing measures of the *Andante* on D, which is unified by the grief motif of Tristan.

So far we have outlined the basic variants of the seventh chord based on ter-tian construction. However, a more radical variant occurs as the *Concerto* moves beyond the tertian construction into more contracted intervals. One basic form, the hybrid (Reh. No. 4, m. 8), is elaborated by one non-tertian passing note, G# (B-D-F#-[G#]-A). This passing note implies the presence of an alternate quasi whole tone form (B-D-F#-G#) to the exclusive tertian construction (B-D-F#-A) by permitting another, non-tertian form (F#-Bb-D-E) to manifest itself as Stefi's third leitmotif in Movement II. Hence this is a true process of compression; together with the augmented triad, it implies the presence of an exclusive whole tone collection. The third leitmotif of Stefi (E-D-Bb-F#) in the second movement, which distorts the hybrid form (B-D-F#-[G#]-A), is the most prominent both structurally and sonically. [Ex. 6]

Example 6 (Movement II, Rehearsal 12, m. 10)

---

217 See Kárpáti, 137–158, for yet another idea of "Variation," in which he uses the term "mistuning" to apply to the identity in the variants, but now with mutations. This is directly relevant here since the perfect fifth contained in the seventh chord is first compressed to a tritone, then to the total chromatic form, and it is precisely the rela-tion of the fifth and octave to the tritone that lies at the base of Kárpáti's concept.

Hence this theme is a fusion of both pentatonic and whole tone. Taken together, it represents something new: from "Strauss" (tertian content) through the chromatic tunnel of the x-cell (Tristan catalyst) and whole tone re-expansion, Bartók moves toward the ideal, but this time in C.

This hidden realm of C, a whole step below the original D, becomes central to the entire work. After an intervallically contracted area (Movement I, mm. 3–4), the cyclic-interval contraction brings us to the tightest part of the tunnel, E-F-F#-G, which then opens out to the new world of folk pentatony. Within this, the cadential figure (B-A-G-E-D-C-G-A, mm. 6–7) contains a hidden transposition (C-E-G-B) of the opening leitmotif on D. In a sense, the larger unfolding of the G triad serves as an elision between the initial D major-seventh chord (D-F#-A-C#) and the final, hidden C major-seventh chord (C-E-G-B). This gives us in descending outline C#-A-F#-D/B-G-E-C, which foreshadows the final shift from the original leitmotivic reference to the final contextual transformation of the still-preserved original leitmotivic identity. This constitutes the global gestalt of the *Concerto*.

All elements from the fugue subject are present and formally unified in the coda. [**Ex. 7**] Here Bartók goes forward: the A minor-seventh chord eventually arrives at the C major. In the fugue subject, we first landed on C major and then moved into A minor. But here at the end it is reversed: departing from the embedded ideal D major-seventh chord within its own resolution, it resolves into the C major-seventh chord. This is the opposite of what happened in the opening fugue subject, where the "C major realm" was cryptic and lacking the potential to reach the *Concerto's* destination.

Example 7 (Coda)

8 Chain of Thirds as Nonfunctional Vehicle for Leitmotivic Progression

Style and process are the essence of Chapters Seven and Eight, which view the exclusivity and metamorphosis of the leitmotif, as well as its progression based on a chain of thirds that interlocks seventh chords as the result of diatonic and pentatonic fusion. These technical aspects subsume two independent courses for the leitmotif. The first is the leitmotif itself and its transformations (the major/minor-seventh chord, French-sixth chord, whole tone form, and chromatic expression of Tristan) as a musical focal point that carries far more meaning than simply its proliferation on nearly each page of the score. The second course is the transfigurative change of the tertian harmonic world of Strauss and Wagner through intermediary whole tone and chromatic stages by means of the leitmotif succession and the relations between them.

Once again we need to bring attention to the identity of the Tristan tunnel and its pivotal function between the D major-seventh chord and the lower whole-step transposition, the C major-seventh chord. This can be shown more explicitly in the descending order of the seventh chords themselves: C#-A-F#-D through B-G-E-C.[218] **[Ex. 1]**

Example 1

The notes of Tristan's grief-motif (A-F-E), constitute the F major-seventh chord (F-A-[]-E), which has an F-E boundary. These two notes form an essential element in identifying Tristan's leitmotif.[219] The direction of the entire work descends from the highest note (C#) of the D major-seventh chord (D-F#-A-C#) to the lowest note (G) of the second inversion of the C major seventh-chord

---

218 Also see **Example 5** in Chapter 7, 108.
219 See **Example 2** in Chapter 5, 80 and **Example 2** in Chapter 6, 88.

(C-E-G-B). Again, as it appears in the fugue subject, the ideal of Stefi rises within the diatonic third progression of the leitmotif and the true "voice" of the peasant descends to the Hungarian pentatonic cadence (m.7). As we progress in the descending chain of thirds, we pass through the E minor seventh-chord (E-G-B-D), a relevant link in the process from the ideal to the Tristan tunnel. Thus the chain of thirds underlies the process itself. [**Diagram 4**]

The chain of thirds is also basic to the principle of motivic transformation. It is striking that the ideal motif (D-F#-A-C#) and grief motif (F-A-[]-E) are equivalent in interval-class structure but different in interval construction. The major-seventh of the ideal motif (D-C#) is transformed into the minor-second (F-E) of Tristan's grief motif (thus the chain of thirds serves as a link in the compression process), but as it appears now it is not the same theme. It is a different theme but the same seventh chord with the articulated minor second (F-E) of grief. This half-step is in the x-cell tetrachord (E-E#-F#-G) of the tunnel.[220] The pivot-note A is part of both extremes: the ideal (F-A-[]-E) and the purification of Tristan's grief (A-F-E).

The new aspect of the same process of motivic transformation, but on a higher architectonic level, is supported within the local architectonic level by the end of the fugue subject (m. 6) where the cadential melodic contour descends: B-A-G-E-D-C-G-A-F. This transformation of the thematic motif into the C-major area (B-G-E-C) is important in that it brings Stefi's ideal (D-F#-A-C#) closer to Tristan's grief (F-A-[]-E) by means of the chain of thirds. One can go even further and recognize the grief-motif as another thematic idea–yet recognized within the

---

220 See Sándor Veress, "Bartók's *Bluebeard's Castle*," *Tempo 13* (1949), 32–38. The chromatic tetrachord also emerges in the First Door of *Bluebeard's Castle* (1911) as the "blood" motif, G#-A-A#-[] (2 measures before Reh. No. 34). Strikingly, as Antokoletz further shows in "Bartók's *Bluebeard*: The Sources of Its Modernism," *College Music Symposium 30/1* (Spring 1990), 85ff., this chromatic cell is comprised of two adjacent half steps, a combination which is part of the linking process in connection with the dramatic development, i.e., A#-B is joined with G#-A to give G#-A/A#-B, two half steps in a 1:1 interval ratio. In his *Musical Symbolism in the Operas of Debussy and Bartók*, Antokoletz clarifies that the A#-B is joined with the other adjacent half-step, B#-C#, which emerges as the boundary of Stefi's (Judith's) original leitmotif, C#-E-G#-B#. As shown in the discussion of the fugue subject **Example 5** in Chapter 7, the inversion (Bb-G-Eb-B) of the original leitmotif, C#-E-G#-B# (m3-M3-M3), is the descending form of the major-seventh chord, B-Eb-G-Bb (based on intervals M3-M3-m3). This inversion (Bb-G-Eb-B) of the original form appears already in measure 3 in the approach to the "tunnel" (the chromatic tetrachord, cell-x).

Whole Tone 0	X cell even	Whole Tone Relation of 7th Chords	X cell odd	Whole Tone 1
		B#		
G#		G#		
		E#		
		C#		C#
		A#		
F#		F#		
		D#		
		B		B keys
		G#		
E	A	E		
	G#	C#		
		A	D	A
		F#	C#	
D	G	D Major 7th	romantic	
	F#	B		
		G		G
		E minor 7th		
C	F Tristan	C		
	E grief	A minor 7th	pentatonic	
		F elision F-A	C-E	F Y5
		D		
Bb		Bb		
		G		
Ab				

Diagram 4

substance from the beginning of the *Concerto*. The violin note A and cadential Subject 2 segment (F-E) refer precisely to the major-seventh chord (F-A-[ ]-E) at that point of elision as something special. However, the shape now is not that of Stefi's leitmotif. It is the major seventh-chord that elides with the minor-seventh chord: F-A-C-E, A-C-E-G, and C-E-G-B together form F-A-C-E-G-B.

There are two levels that significantly present themselves in this identification: motivic pitch relations and thematic identity. The pitch relations are based on the progression of minor and major thirds. Within the systematic process of expansion/compression, which is constantly reiterated and varied on all levels, the chain of thirds becomes more abstract as it compresses into a chromatic four-note segment in its original identity of x-cell (E-E#-F#-G). This final form at the outset of the main fugue subject bridges the gap between the two opposite worlds: both the chain of thirds is a link in the compression process, and the x-cell is conversely a link in the process of expansion. Both are part of the same concept. Both serve as links between the two poles of the ideal world of the beloved and the true world of the peasant. And both the "Tristan" and "Stefi" themes are one, but the *one* is not the themes themselves–it is the unique material from which both themes come. Thus Stefi's ideal is transformed into Tristan's anguish, while both are based on the same structure in which the pitch material and the interval structure are related. As a result, two levels may be discerned: the process from D to C that governs the whole *Concerto*, and the chromatic x-cell segment that becomes a tunnel within its catalytic function. The link and holding frame for both these levels is the chain of thirds as presented in the descending contour of the fugue subject. In this descent, one perceives and comes to know the beauty and profound message that is meant to be discovered.

The center of Movement II represents the focal point of the *Concerto* at the highest architectonic level of the transformational process between the two worlds. As Bartók himself tells us, a new theme (Reh. Nos. 12 and 13) articulates the succession of Stefi's leitmotifs.[221] We acknowledge here a thematic motif (E-D-B^b-F$^{\#}$) within the boundary of the E-F$^{\#}$ minor seventh.[222] Although this chord is a whole tone mutation of the diatonic seventh-chord construction, it nevertheless belongs to the process of unfolding third transpositions. As we have already shown, the entire chain is nothing but alternations between the major-seventh chord and pentatonic minor-seventh chord (Stefi's "ideal," D-F$^{\#}$-A-C$^{\#}$, which initiates the chain and has a major-seventh boundary, D-C$^{\#}$, and A-C-E-G, which ends the fugue subject and has a minor-seventh boundary, A-G). While the minor-seventh boundary (F$^{\#}$-E) of the new leitmotif implies the presence of the pentatonic or minor-seventh chord stage of the chain, E-D-B^b-F$^{\#}$ (Reh. No. 12, m. 11), the inner notes (B^b-D) of E-D-B^b-F$^{\#}$ produce a mutation that draws the whole tone boundary into the whole tone sphere. The result is a hybrid construction that takes us away from the diatonic tertian forms of the leitmotif and produces a construction in the upper two notes (D-E) of what originally would have been the interval of a third, D^b-F (in the hypothetical transposition, G^b-B^b-D^b-F). Thus we distinguish a descending melodic contour of E-D-B^b-F$^{\#}$ as representing the whole tone intermediary stage in the process of transformation. [Ex. 2]

---

221 Béla Bartók, *Briefe an Stefi Geyer*, 44.
222 See *Béla Bartók Letters*, Demény, 87.

Example 2 (Rehearsal No. 12, m. 9 and Rehearsal No. 13, mm. 1–4, Solo Violin)

Since this lyrical theme cannot be proven to be a pure diatonic theme based on thirds, we should rather consider the first interval of the major third, F#-A# (in enharmonic spelling F#-Bb), as combined with another major third, Db-F (in enharmonic spelling, C#-E#). Interval C#-E# is no less than a symmetrical expansion of the major-second D-E from the motif as it actually occurs and brings us to the major-third transposition F#-A#-[C#-E#] of Stefi's original seventh-chord (D-F#-A-C#). Or one can look further ahead and attribute the tritone transposition to the goal-oriented C major-seventh chord. However, with D-E the tetrachord F#-Bb-[D-E] functions here as a hybridized form. The D turns the ideal motif into the whole tone collection. Stefi's new non-diatonic leitmotif, E-D-Bb-F#, with the upbeat G#-A#, provides us with an expanded segment, F#-G#-A#-D-E, which belongs exclusively to the whole tone area. Furthermore, the segment that follows the cadential figure of the ritard, which itself arises from an implied x-cell (G#-A-A#-B), changes the function of the sustained E. It is drawn into a new intervallic phase articulated by the new theme. As a result, we encounter a more radical phase in the musical language spoken in the *Concerto*: whole tone. Whole-step D-E induces an intermediary stage based on the major second (minor seventh, E-F#) of the minor-seventh chord and the major thirds (F#-Bb and Bb-D) of the major-seventh chord. Thus the whole tone variant of the leitmotif becomes hybrid since it combines elements from both forms. The whole-step on top of the descending motif belongs to the third variant (B-D-[F#-G#]-A) of Stefi's leitmotif. [**Ex. 2**]

It is striking that the order of events at this thematic juncture, which reinterprets the E as part of the whole tone event, is a reversal of the contraction-expansion within the opening fugue subject–x to whole-tone at the pivotal E, versus whole tone to x. We thus arrive at the point that confirms the relation between the macrocosmic and microcosmic levels of the entire composition, an issue that was posed from the very beginning.

This central thematic manifestation of Stefi's leitmotif in Movement II (Reh. Nos. 12 and 13) is precisely the structural point at which the process of contraction begins. In this compositional momentum to which we are subjected, we are forced to respond to this major change in Bartók's conception that appears in his move toward motivic transformation. Two other important questions also need to be addressed: how the hybrid form reflects the beginning of the *Concerto*, and what it completes at the end.

Stefi's new leitmotif is a momentous signal for Béla's crossroad that allows him to look back to the beginning–the ideal of Stefi. But he cannot leave it there. Her newly transformed leitmotif (non-diatonic variant) gives him the impulse to move forward. The composer finds the way that takes both Béla and Stefi into the new world of the ideal: the domain of C. The gap (D-B^b) in the four-note motif of the hybrid form of Stefi's ideal, E-D-[]-B^b-F$^\sharp$, is formed by the absence of the C note within the whole tone trajectory. The first two notes (B^b-A^b) of the tritone transposition of the theme (Reh. No. 13, m. 4) extend the hybrid form of Stefi's leitmotif to E-D-[]-B^b-A^b-F$^\sharp$. As we recall, the whole tone segment from the fugue subject, B-C$^\sharp$-D$^\sharp$-E$^\sharp$, referred to as y-cell, points to whole-tone 1. However, at the midpoint of the *Concerto*, Bartók prepares the domain of C by shifting to the other whole tone cycle (WT-O) in the new leitmotif, thus looking to the end of his journey as the completion for both the composer and the "Béla-Tristan" hero.

But there is only one way for him to go in order to reach his "harbor." Similar to what had preceded the tunnel (x-cell) in the opening fugue subject, the composer again goes through the y-cell, the whole tone phase. However, this time the latter is not a y-cell but a larger whole tone segment. The foremost event here is the reappearance and completion of the whole tone scale at the coda (Reh. No. 34, mm. 1–2). The C note–the missing element of the newly defined leitmotif as a non-diatonic tetrachord (E-D-Bb-F$^\sharp$)–is now expressed. However, it is the whole tone 1 scale, the one from the opening fugue subject, that is inevitably present at the concluding point. This momentary return creates an ambiguity in expectation because it sparks our memory of how the *Concerto* began. Nevertheless, it creates the sense of something new, for it is the beginning–the very first moment of the *Concerto*–that also marks its end. Bartók completes the whole tone scale by expanding the original y tetrachord, B-C$^\sharp$-D$^\sharp$-E$^\sharp$, by its tritone transposition, F-G-A-B, only toward the end of the coda. He achieves this at the same structural point at which he completes his autobiographical work. The original tetrachordal whole tone segment (y-cell) now emerges as part of the larger whole tone structure as a primary foreground event.

Beyond this, the primary goal of the entire process of transformation is connected in the converse relation of the D and C transpositions of the leitmotif. While one (D) was pure and unobscured as foreground arpeggiation (D-F#-A-C#), the other (C) was hidden by scalar embellishment (B̲-A-G̲-E-D-C̲-G-A). Conversely, the latter emerges at the *Lento* (Reh. No. 34, m. 2) as an unembellished ascending arpeggiation (C-E-G-B), while the original ideal on D is now embedded in the obsessive verbunkos figuration of the rapid friss style (Reh. No. 33).

Part of the same perception is the presence of another transpositional level, this time on G. It is again in the chain of thirds that the G major-seventh chord clearly emerges as Stefi's ideal, not as a single line of the initiating solo violin but separated in the texture by a wood instrument (clarinet) and orchestra. In the fugue subject the G major-seventh chord was subordinate to the other seventh-chord transposition rather than asserting its own identity. The G major-seventh chord (Reh. No. 34), now with D# (G-B-D#-F#), still reflects the main (ideal) leit-motif. This new whole tone detail (G-B-D#-[]) permits a hybrid construction that results in the thematic contour of the third non-diatonic form of Stefi's leit-motif. The D# and F# of the G-seventh variant refer to the jagged virtuoso theme (D#-F#-A#-C-E) that opens Movement II, in which the D# is the only non-whole tone element, and G-B-F# structurally refers to the original diatonic form of the leitmotif. It is in the interplay of these subsets (diatonic and whole tone) that the basic process of the work is now reflected.

A special relationship (D/D#) is established between the conclusion of the *Concerto* and the fugue subject. The D#, the first note of Movement II, directly follows the tonic note of the rising D major-seventh chord that ends Movement I. This relation in the succession between the two notes (D and D#) changes at the end of the *Concerto* as D# replaces D in the altered G-B-D#-F# leitmotif (Reh. No. 34). D# stands for the D in the original form, G-B-D-F#. At the same time, as D# replaces D, the new whole tone 1 vocabulary takes precedence by its comple-tion at the end of the *Concerto* (Reh. No. 34). The second function of the D#, i.e., as whole tone 1 component, is suggested by its unique position in the passage as the only element outside of the whole tone 0 segment ([]-F#-A#-C-E). At that point (Movement II, mm. 1–3), D# was linearly directed to E of the C major-seventh chord transposition. At the end of the *Concerto*, this leading function of D# seems to be the same since the E♭ (in enharmonic spelling, D#) of whole tone 1 scale is succeeded directly by the final C-E-G-B ascent. In other words, the D# to E of the opening jagged form foreshadows the overall progression to the domain of the ideal C.

The D#, however, does not disappear by its resolution to the C major-seventh chord. The *Concerto* ends with a C-minor chord, in which the minor third (E♭) replaces the major third (E) of the ideal on C. The D# was the first note of the jagged five-note motif, D#-F#-A#-C-E, which contains the French sixth chord (F#-A#-C-E). The latter belongs to both octatonic and whole tone spheres simultaneously, that is, to a common segment between these two collections. This is confirmed by a comparison of measures 1–2 with measures 15–16, where the D# is notated as Eb in the more extended form of the motif. The latter ends with an explicit foreground occurrence of the C-minor triad, a premonition of the *Concerto's* cadenza.

In the final analysis, it is Eb/D# that is missing in the opening fugue subject–perhaps the D# from Tristan's grief, A-F-E-[D#], which is the three-note form that is never completed anywhere in the *Concerto*. In other words, we have A-F-E at measure 7, and A-Bb-B at Rehearsal No. 2, measures 1–2. These two separate Tristan references never connect with D#. Indeed, D# is an "odd" element everywhere in terms of the whole tone sphere, for instance, in D#/F#-A#-C-E and G-B-D#-F#. In the final measures of the *Concerto*, the only significance that can be imputed to the Eb in the C-minor triad (C-Eb-G) is the funereal mood in the *First String Quartet* and, just a few years later, in *Bluebeard's Castle*. The cadential chord, C-Eb-G, is only the end of the *Concerto's* score, but not the end of the message.

Epilogue

Is a concerto simply a concerto because a composer calls it such? In the case of Bartók's *1907 Violin Concerto* this is not a contrived question, and for three reasons. First, unlike the traditional concertos of the eighteenth and nineteenth centuries, it has only two movements, not three. It is not surprising, then, that Stefi Geyer considered the work as a fantasy.[223] In her 1953 interview with Denis Dille, she confirmed this classification: "I believe that Bartók hasn't kept a copy of the *Concerto*. It is not a concerto in the proper sense, but rather a Fantasy for Violin and Orchestra. The theme of the first movement seems to portray my person and express my character."[224] Second, genre names categorize musical compositions and thus help to condition our expectations and responses–yet the musical structure of the *Concerto* is unconventional. The first movement does not follow the typical sonata-concerto form but is rather generated by a fugal process (see Chapter 6). And the second movement, with its formal overlaps of ritornello/rondo/sonata-allegro forms, comes closer to the traditional model of a third movement, which is usually in sonata or rondo form. Finally, it is typically the last movement that serves as the vehicle for the composer to offer the soloist the best opportunity for displaying virtuoso brilliance. But in contrast to all of the last movements of the violin concertos that constituted the standard repertory of virtuosos at that time, Bartók's *Allegro giocoso* denies the soloist "the last word," ending instead with a brief orchestral ritornello that totally reverses the mood of the soloist's final cadenza statement.

In light of the genesis of the work (see Chapter 5), we now know why Bartók specifically wanted to write a concerto. His choice of genre was the result of his having fallen in love with the violinist Stefi Geyer. We also know why the work turned out as unconventional as it is. A composer compelled to create a work that follows an individual path will not choose a form that constrains his intentions. As stated earlier in Chapter 6, it became an "absolutely unconditional necessity" for Bartók that Stefi's piece would only have two movements: "Two contrasting pictures: that is all."[225] Furthermore, in order to communicate the composer's intimate, passionate, and finally disillusioned experiences, the *Concerto* bears

---

223 An argument could also be made for a relation with the Lisztian-type genre of rhapsody that manifests the Csárdás-like features.

224 See Dille, "Angaben zum Violinkonzert 1907," 92.

225 Béla Bartók, *Briefe an Stefi Geyer*, no. 21 (21 December 1907), sec. 7.

a quasi-narrative sub-text with the polarity of two strata: the purely musical and the allusively poetic, both inspired by his love for Stefi. An overpowering wealth of individual expression is the result. The stress of motivic and thematic metamorphosis that characterizes the two movements of the *Concerto* colors the intrinsic meaning of each movement in its progress. It is the way in which Bartók calls attention to the thematic changes or the order in which they occur that invites us to think of the work in terms of a poetic narrative.

When it comes to verbal interpretation of music, we encounter the difficulty of introducing a parallel language alongside the music itself in the work of interpretation. And not only parallel but perhaps primary, for is it really possible without words to communicate an intellectual understanding of anything? Words enjoy an unchallenged supremacy over all other modes of communication since they mirror ideas, and ideas are capable of representing the forms, more or less adequately, of all realities. But reality is more than the communication of intelligibility, and music presents reality in ways that include but also surpass intelligibility. Moreover, this argument with respect to relative superiority is ineluctably one-sided because words here are enlisted in their own defense while no music is heard through these sentences. And music's cause suffers from the liability that we cannot musically document this competition between musical reality and reflection on it. For this reason, it seems safest to adopt a stance of complementarity by recognizing the unique contributions of musical reality and verbal reflection, and to insist that words in the precise task of musical interpretation are the servant and not the master of the sounds.

If music cannot adjudicate words, it can at least mimic them by way of musical intelligibility. To narrate is to tell a story. To write a story is to depict and evoke a sense of what has happened, to relate what is transpiring at a particular moment. The plot thickens when one wrestles with the question of narrativity and music. We know, of course, that linguistic-narrative structure cannot be duplicated in music, for music knows no "grammatical" past, present, or future. Indeed, its hold on the past and the future is tenuous because one cannot transcend what one is confined within, for music is in perpetual motion in a way that a text is not. Even if the reader reads a text in time, the text stands over against the reader such that page 15 is present in the same moment as page 250. But the score is not the concerto, for the concerto exists when it is played and what is played. It naturally lives in the here and now of the ever changing *nunc stans*, and it exists as the sum total of its many performances.

And yet, like a narrative, a musical work is able to gather up the past fragments and retain them in the components of this now, this present moment, and the heritage of this moment reflects what has gone before. What was, is now–but in a different way. Is it not for that very reason that we have no difficulty experiencing the "plot," for example, of Beethoven's *Fifth Symphony*, even without words? The work moves from darkness to light, and we move with it as enlightened–as well as with the tradition led by "those who know" and have helped us to "see the light" of right interpretation. With Beethoven's *Sixth*, the music is accompanied by words–the composer's programmatic titles for the five movements–so that the whole work is now the score, the titles, and the actual performance.

In regard to Bartók's *1907 Concerto*, we stand between music without explicit verbal interpretation (Beethoven's *Fifth*) and music with such interpretation (Beethoven's *Sixth*). A "textual tradition" stands behind the *Concerto*, but the words are hidden, cryptic, elusive, and the music that "speaks" them is abstruse and complex, as our study has shown. Those who have been able to peer behind the curtains will experience and understand the "story" of Bartók's *1907 Concerto* that speaks of Béla and Stefi at each moment of a composition that gathers into the present what has preceded it and takes it where it has not yet gone. In this sense, the *Concerto* possesses a hidden key of interpretation locked away in Stefi's desk. Without this key, the work *is* the self-standing music as performed; with this key, the work *is* the music plus its verbal interpretation. Because one hears the music in a different way after reading Bartók's letters of 1907 and 1908, we become more complete listeners after we learn that this work began with written words that identified its motifs and their meaning. And then when one returns to hear the *Concerto*, one replays Bartók's written words with a new depth. But even here we run up against the disadvantage of only one correspondent being represented in the annals of recorded history. Stefi's responses are sparse indeed and mostly lost to us.

Who was Béla Bartók when he composed the *Concerto*? In our narrative chapters depicting "Bela and Stefi," we suggested the answer that he was both "poet and peasant." As poet, he was a member of the intellectual elite, a writer of words and of art music. As peasant, he associated with a simpler world in his longing for the depth of its "natural naïveté" and the strength of its musical roots.

Does "poetic" imply "romantic?" Ludwig Tieck had strict criteria: he considered Robert Schumann's settings of Robert Burns's poems brimming with such passions as joy, sorrow, and rejection as insufficient evidence for labeling them "romantic." He rendered a similar verdict on the music of Carl Loewe, Johannes Brahms, and Ernst Wilhelm Wolf. On the other hand, E. T. A. Hoffmann is spokesman for many when he calls music "the most romantic of all the arts. . . for only the infinite is its subject." In our search for a little more definition, we note that the question of calling a composer romantic is tied to time, style, and individual perception. And to speak of a "romantic" work is to make a much stronger claim then to simply speak of a "romantic" composer. "One of the first things most people want to hear discussed in relation to composing is the question of inspiration," notes Aaron Copland.

> Nor must we forget the influence of the romantic movement. It wasn't enough for a romantic composer to write a sad piece; he wanted you to know who it was that felt sad and the circumstances of his sadness. Debussy's only opera *Pélléas et Mélisande*, in method of feelings was the antithesis of Wagnerian music drama. In Wagner's opera *Tristan*, when the lovers declare themselves for the first time, there is an outpouring of the emotions in music, but when Pélléas and Mélisande first declare their love for each other, there is complete silence. Everyone–singers, orchestra, and composer–is overcome with emotions.[226]

From an awareness of Bartók's musical and aesthetic goals, as evidenced both in his correspondence with Geyer and in his compositional choices in the *Concerto*, one cannot help but appraise the *1907 Violin Concerto* from a "romantic" perspective in Copland's sense, at least in its first movement.

The question of the romantic character of the *Concerto* must also be placed in a multidisciplinary, or perhaps we should rather say, a "multi-domain" context. At the turn of the century in central Europe, there was an enormous confluence of the various arts, and perhaps no other epoch so manifested this interrelationship as a virtual necessity. In fact, a correspondence among the various arts became almost an aesthetic postulate.[227] The young Bartók expressed this in his own unique way through a linkage of music, philosophy, and personal experience. Frigyesi observes that through his personal experience, Bartók synthesized a fundamental aspect of Nietzsche's world consciousness:

> He who really could participate [in the others' fortunes and sufferings] would have to despair of the value of life... for mankind has as a whole no goal, and the individual man when he regards its total course cannot derive from it any support or comfort, but must be reduced to despair. If in all he does he has before him the ultimate goallessness of man, his actions acquire in his own eyes the character of useless squandering. But to feel thus "squandered," not merely as an individual but as humanity as a whole, in the way we behold the individual fruits of nature squandered, is a feeling beyond all other

---

226 Aaron Copland, *What to Listen for in Music* (The New American Library: McGraw-Hill, 1039), 142.

227 Frigyesi's *Béla Bartók and Turn-of-the-Century Budapest* (op. cit.) is a comprehensive study of this aesthetic achievement.

feelings. –But who is capable of such feeling? Certainly only a poet: and poets always know how to console themselves.[228]

Béla Bartók was a poet as well. It was his images of and love for Geyer that inspired the genesis of the *Concerto*, and it was her rejection of his love that not only marked the end of their relationship but also sealed the fate of the composition. It was never to be published and never to be performed during his lifetime. However, as we now know, Stefi's leitmotif, which gives the first movement its identity, continued to serve as a quasi-ideal motif for several other of his works (1907–1911), thus bringing about a quasi-dramatic-poetic unity among them. This transference of materials of the *Concerto* among these contemporaneous works is unique in all of Bartók's oeuvre in that the same material was given many different contextual settings, each with its own poetic meaning. And this suggests a new question: what does this tell us about the composer and his attitude about his work? As an answer we suggest a hypothesis based on our interpretation of the facts as we understand them.

It was especially the leitmotif, implicitly identified with his idealized Stefi, that Bartók reused in other compositions. The first movement of the *Concerto* was preserved by converting it into the first movement of his *Two Portraits* (for orchestra), op. 5. By saving this music, it therefore appears that he wanted to enshrine the idealized state of his own feelings rather than simply retain a memory of Stefi. Perhaps this was also a way of allowing the *Concerto* to remain hidden and yet offer its treasures to the world at the same time. To support this thesis, it is telling that Bartók did not plunder the *Concerto's* second movement, which he identified with the lovely, witty, and real Stefi, for the second movement of his *Two Portraits*, but appropriated his *Bagatelle No. 14* instead. The theme of the *Concerto's* second movement, the jagged theme of the "real" Stefi–the virtuoso–reappears only in one other work, his *First String Quartet* (1908–1909), at the beginning and at the climax of the first movement (*fortissimo*, seven measures before the pianissimo ending). Elliott Antokoletz observes that

> "[Bartók's] apprehension that the love between Stefi and himself would be dissolved was soon to be realized, and he expressed his feelings about this by his eventual transformation of the lively, "witty and amusing" second-movement theme of the *Violin Concerto...* into the slow fugue theme that opens the *First String Quartet* (1907–1909)."[229]

---

228 Frigyesi, 154. Quotations from Friedrich Nietzsche's *Human, All Too Human: A Book for Free Spirits*, trans. R. J. Hollingdale, 7th ed. (Cambridge; Cambridge University Press, 1993), 29, 30; original emphasis.

229 Antokoletz, *Musical Symbolism*, 210.

Because Stefi rejected his romantic feelings, Bartók finishes the *Concerto* as he did. Its conclusion is abrupt and inevitable. But both its thematic transformation and his emotional collapse continue in the *Quartet's* opening melody that unfolds the seventh chord (F-Ab-C-E), which is the minor duller variant of Stefi's ideal leitmotif. She herself comments:

> In our correspondence, which I am keeping, he [Bartók] gave out two or three themes that relate to my person. The two [*Concerto*] movements are two portraits: the first is one of the young girl he loved; the second is the violinist he admired. Please note that the first theme of the Second Movement is also the first theme of the Quartet. Bartók himself brought this to my attention in his last letter when he wrote to me: "I have started a quartet; the first theme is the theme of the Second Movement: it is my 'funeral dirge.'"[230]

Antokoletz observes here that the "duality of emotions spans the gamut from love to the emptiness of death."[231] The absolute result of Bartók's relationship with Stefi in terms of unfulfilled love is symbolized in the movement from the ideal identification in the first movement of the *Violin Concerto* (D-F$^{\#}$-A-C$^{\#}$/ M3-m3-M3) to the funeral transformation in the first movement of the *First String Quartet* (F-Ab-C-E/ m3-M3-M3), as well as in Judith's vocal sound in *Bluebeard's Castle* (Gb-A-Db-Eb-F/m3-M3-[M2]-M3) by way of the theme in the *Concerto's* second movement delineating Stefi's character. More specifically, B-D-F$^{\#}$-A (m3-M3-m3) is the link between the ideal (M3-m3-M3), which alternates within the chain, and the form of Bartók's "funeral dirge," F-A^{b}-C-E (m3-M3-M3), in connection with the *First String Quartet*. The latter sequence (m3-M3-M3) stands outside of the diatonic chain of thirds and leads us into the whole tone world because of its two adjacent major thirds.

Having earlier identified and discussed this variant of Stefi's leitmotif in the score of the *Concerto*, we may now acknowledge its legacy as prominent in Bartók's works in 1907–1911. This minor-seventh chord, B-D-F$^{\#}$-A (m3-M3-m3) represents a stage of compression stemming from the larger intervals of the original major-seventh chord, D-F$^{\#}$-A-C$^{\#}$ (M3-m3-M3/Stefi's love motif). The intrusion of G$^{\#}$ induces an intermediary stage of the minor-seventh m3-M3-m3 chord and of the major-seventh chord M3-m3-M3. The whole-step on top of the descending motif belongs to the third variant (B-D-[F$^{\#}$-G$^{\#}$]-A) of Stefi's leitmotif. Thus the leitmotif becomes a hybrid that borrows components from both forms. It is hybrid because it combines the major third (D-F$^{\#}$) of the major-seventh

---

230 See Denijs Dille, "Angaben zum Violinkonzert 1907," 92. See also János Kárpáti, *Bartók's String Quartets*, 173.

231 Antokoletz, *Musical Symbolism*, 210.

sonore

Example 1 [232]

form of Stefi's ideal with the minor thirds (B-D and F#-A) of the pentatonic minor-seventh chord of the Hungarian peasant. And it contains a passing note (G#), a raised sixth, that allows a whole tone detail to emerge, which is so essential to the sense of mood transformation. [**Ex. 1**]

Hence the pentatonic modality becomes an important link between the Straussian harmony and whole-tone (D-F#-G#). The transcendent quality of this hybrid form and its melodic tendency saddened and contracted at its lower third (m3-M3-M3) indeed contains the seeds for the new world of the whole tone transformation.

Bartók's compositional creativity between the *Violin Concerto* and the *String Quartet No. 1* was channeled into piano music that included a number of significant character pieces published under such titles as *Bagatelles, Ten Easy Piano Pieces, Seven Sketches, Burlesques,* and *Two Elegies.* Of these, the *Bagatelle No. 13* ("Elle est morte"), "A Portrait of a Girl" (from *Seven Sketches*), and the *Second Elegy* deserve our attention. Victoria Fisher offers an important remark on *Bagatelle No. 13* [**Ex. 2**]:

> The significance of the title and use of the leitmotiv in this piece is especially fascinating, in light of the direct resemblance it bears to the example used by Bartók to introduce the motive to Geyer in his letter of September 1907. Both versions of the leitmotiv use dotted-rhythm triads in the accompaniment, to create a ponderous, dirge like mood. The leitmotiv appears in the same transposition, although in different guises: the fragment from the letter in the minor version, the Bagatelle no. 13 in an enharmonically spelled major version, D♭-F-A♭-C... [T]here is no doubt that the original intention of this funereal piano piece, with its mournful violinistic melodic line, was to express Bartók's sadness for the loss of Stefi Geyer.[233]

---

232 In the *Concerto's* score Rehearsal No. 4, m. 5.
233 Victoria Fischer, 273.

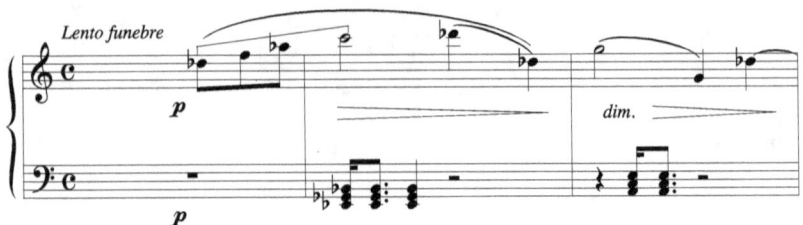

Example 2 (*Bagatelle No. 13*)

Dorothy Lamb Crawford depicts *Bagatelle No. 14* [**Ex. 3**] as "a bitter, demented waltz, in which the motive is hurled about in a nightmarish whirl akin to the transformation of Berlioz's idée-fixe in the *Symphonie fantastique*."[234]

Example 3 (*Bagatelle No. 14*)
Valse: ma mie qui danse

What about his "A Portrait of a Girl" from the *Seven Sketches*? Whose portrait is it? The answer appears easy enough since the piece is dedicated to Márta Ziegler, at that time his pupil and soon to be first wife. And yet this answer does not fully satisfy because it does not explain the change of mood toward the end of the piece and its unmistakable reference to the sonority of Stefi's leitmotif in the form of the vertical D-major seventh chord. [**Ex. 4**] Stefi herself concluded that it is her leitmotif, that it refers to her, and that it signifies no one else: "That he used it in '*Ma mie qui danse*' [D-F#-A-C# leitmotif, the theme of the *Concerto's* first movement] seems to confirm this and shows a reaction after our breaking up."[235] First heard in measure 3, it then appears more significantly at the change of

---

234 Ibid.; Crawford, "Love and Anguish," 130–131.
235 See Denijs Dille, "Angaben zum Violinkonzert 1907," 92.

tempo from *Andante* to *Poco meno mosso, poco espressivo*. Three measures before the piece ends, the D-major seventh chord appears again, but now resolved into G major instead of G[#] minor–a resolution strangely disappointing to us who know.[236]

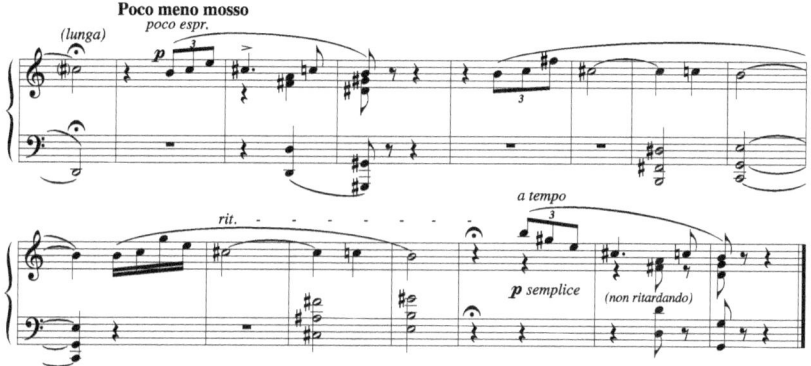

Example 4 ("A Portrait of a Girl," mm. 50 to the end)

The main motif (A-G-F-D-B) of the *Second Elegy* of 1909 also recalls a leitmotif from the *1907 Violin Concerto*, namely the so-called second theme (E-D-B♭-F#, melodically descending) of the second movement. [**Ex. 5**] Its intervallic boundary (A-B) is the minor seventh rather than the initial major seventh (G-A♭). This is the "Theme 3" that Bartók quotes in his letter of September 20, 1907, and that he identifies with Stefi (Theme 1 is Stefi's leitmotif from Movement I, Theme 2 is Stefi's leitmotif from Movement II).

Bartók's abundant reuse of various themes in the *Concerto* may ultimately indicate the musical autonomy of the work in contradistinction to its concrete extramusical subject, his beloved Stefi, that motivated his original composition. Or perhaps, intended or unintended, it was a testament to the fact that his beloved,

---

236 When Kenneth Chalmers, *Béla Bartók* (London: Phaidon Press, 1995), 77 states that "Stefi's motif, upside-down is the final seemingly inconsonant phrase of the piece," he seems to refer to the melodically descending minor-seventh chord (B-G#-E-C#) in measures 62–63. However he appears to mistake the identifying parameter of what Bartók himself first called Stefi's leitmotif (see Chapters 2–5), which is always the interval of the major seventh. The boundary of the minor seventh occurs only in the so-called second theme (E-D-Bb-F#, melodically descending) of the second movement of the *Concerto*, which Bartók quotes in his letter of September 20, 1907. It is this motivic configuration which Bartók uses in his second *Elegy*. [**Example 5**]

Example 5 (*Second Elegy*)

by leaving an indelible mark on his heart, thereby left an inerasable impress on his music. Either way, the *Concerto* embraces the "infinity" referred to by E.T.A. Hoffmann in his essay on Beethoven's instrumental music ("absolute music").[237] The *1907 Violin Concerto* is thus the door that opens up to Bartók's masterworks.

Béla Bartók himself stated that his music is a biography of sorts (see Chapter 1). He takes this insight further and speaks about the real and the true artist in his letter to Márta and Hermina Ziegler on February 4, 1909:

> It is strange that in music the basis of motivation has so far been only enthusiasm, love sorrow, or at most despair–that is, only the so-called lofty feelings. It is only in our times that there has been a place for the painting of the feeling of vengeance, the grotesque, and the sarcastic. For this reason the music of today could be called realist because, unlike the idealism of the previous eras, it extends with honesty to all human emotions without excluding any. In the last century, there were only sporadic examples for this, for instance, in Berlioz's *Symphonie Fantastique*, Liszt's *Faust*, Wagner's *Meistersinger*, and Strauss's *Heldenleben*.[238]

This assertion is particularly applicable to his creations of his first masterwork period (1907–1911). We already know that prior to his work on the *Violin*

---

237 Ernst Theodor Amadeus Hoffmann, "Beethoven's Instrumental Music" in *Source Readings in Music History*, ed. Oliver Strunk (New York: Norton, 1950), 775–781.

238 A letter to Márta and Hermina Ziegler (Darázs, 4 February 1909), in Béla Bartók, Jr., ed., *Bartók Béla családi levelei* [Béla Bartók's family letters] (Budapest: Zeneműkiadó, 1981), 187–188.

Concerto and while appointed as a piano teacher at the Academy of Music in Budapest, Bartók not only continued his folk music investigations, but also methodically studied the music of Debussy, even purchasing numeral copies of the French composer's works.[239] It is during this time that he became attentive to the pentatonic phrases in his own Hungarian folk heritage. But then all of these motivations and stimuli were suddenly interrupted by the shattering outburst and power of his new and deeply felt passion for Stefi Geyer. As we have established in Chapter 5, the subject and melody of unrequited love in Wagner's *Tristan und Isolde* are symbolized in the *Violin Concerto* by the spirit of Tristan. We also know that Bartók's musical language joins that of Wagner's in the fervent bond of *desire* and *grief*, which the score of Stefi's *Concerto* brilliantly supports with manifold musical elements. Antokoletz comments on this: "In accord with Bartók's emotional transformation associated with Stefi, this "love-death" duality (and identity) evolved into the musical forms and symbolic meaning of the motif during the period of compositional creativity extending from the *1907 Violin Concerto* to the *Bluebeard* opera."[240]

In support of this symbolic and autobiographical meaning, we find an intriguing statement in a letter Bartók writes to Stefi at the beginning of 1908: "I have begun a quartet; the first theme is the theme of the second movement [of *1907 Violin Concerto*]: this is my funeral dirge."[241] Antokoletz notes that "it is also significant that the very opening F# pentatonic ("Darkness") theme, which returns at the end of the Bluebeard opera in association with 'endless darkness,' is similar to the theme in the second of Bartók's *Four Dirges for Piano*, op. 8b (1908). Ultimately, it is Bartók's need to control the woman that seems to lie at the heart of the parallel between Stefi and Judith."[242] Since *Bluebeard's Castle* supports this thesis insofar as it is based on a pessimistic approach toward a woman, it is not astonishing that Stefi's leitmotif is the focal point for musical expression. For it was only two years earlier that this young woman rejected the young composer's romantic feelings. But there is a key difference: Stefi's rejection of Bartók is now reversed in this opera featuring only two main characters. Here

---

239 Antokoletz, *Musical Symbolism*, 14, n. 2; Anthony Cross, "Debussy and Bartók," *Musical Times* 108 (1967), 126.

240 Ibid., 211.

241 Denijs Dille, "Angaben zum Violinkonzert 1907, den Deux Portraits, dem Quartett op. 7 und den Zwei Rumänischen Tänzen," 92. See also János Kárpáti, Bartók's String Quartets, 173.

242 Antokoletz, *Musical Symbolism*, 198.

it is the power of Bluebeard's mind and emotions hovering over Judith's personal weakness. Bartók's personal descent into unresponsiveness and loneliness, coupled with the resignation that even a life companion will not bring him full contentment, appears to be reflected in Bluebeard's being led to dissatisfaction with the woman whom he eventually abandons. Antokoletz notes that

> Bartók's letter provides us with a more profound insight into his relationship with Stefi. From this relationship we become aware of significant parallels between Stefi and Judith. Bartók's certainty "that he would be disappointed," even "should he succeed in finding someone," is more evident in the opera, where Judith's prying into Bluebeard's personal life leads him to dissatisfaction with the woman; his abandonment of her, then as he forces her to join his previous wives behind the seventh door, leads to his own eternal loneliness in "endless night," a metaphor for his death.[243]

When we hear the music and know the personal background, we can certainly feel that Bartók's life leaves indelible markings on the score, but let us now provide more technical evidence for this. The following final diagram traces the career of the major seventh chord (M3/M7), showing how its generation of the transpositions and intervallic transformations that are part of the developmental process unifies all of the works these years. Aside from its extra-musical leitmotivic function, the major seventh chord (M3/M7) serves as a generator of variant seventh chords that can be shown to be part of a larger system. Specifically, the diagram systematically reveals all forms of the seventh chord that are diatonic as well as this one important m3/m7 non-diatonic seventh chord. Bartók refers to this chord, which may be considered as the polarized structure of Stefi's ideal form, as his funereal form. In effect, this form represents Stefi's rejection of Béla, or more exactly, his death, and at the end serves as a link from diatonic to non-diatonic–to a dissonant expression of the whole-tone language.

---

243 Ibid.

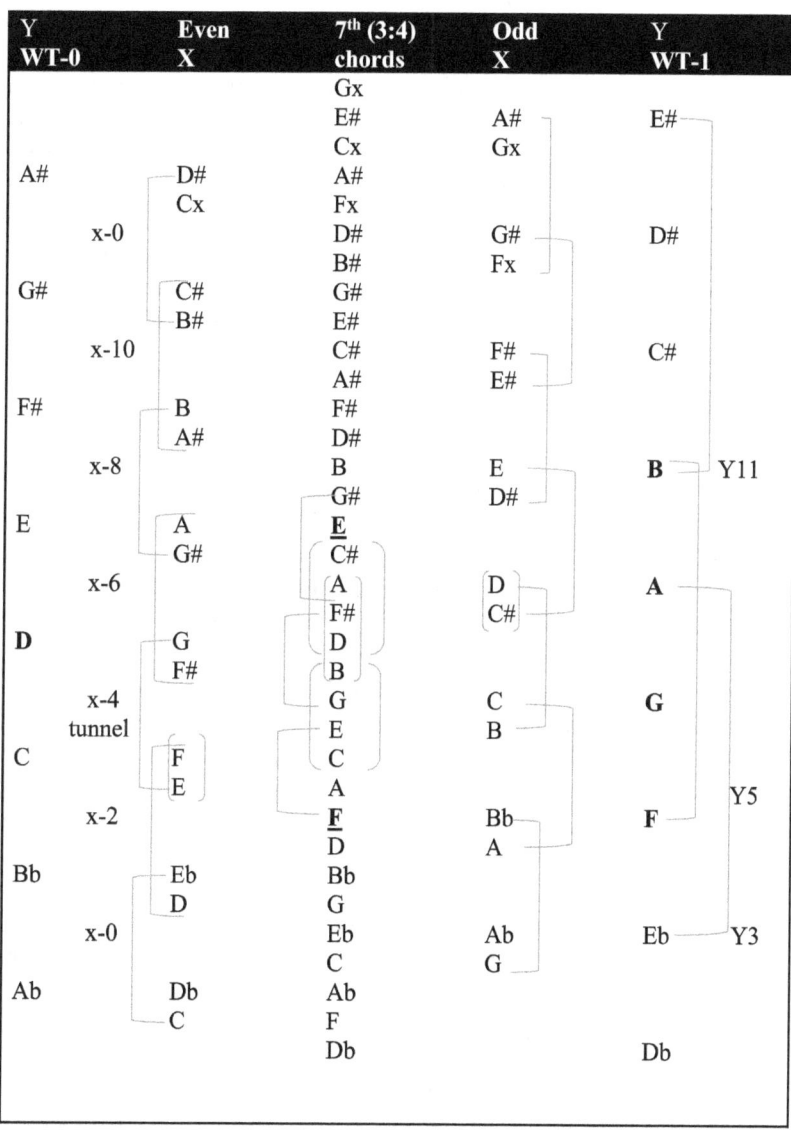

Final Diagram[244]

---

244 Antokoletz, *Musical Symbolism*, 26.

In a sense, this seventh chord system presented here again (see Chapter 8) reflects the overall progression from the pioneering *Violin Concerto* to *Bluebeard's Castle*. At the same time, the progression reflects the internal relations of the opera itself.[245] We are not surprised that Stefi's leitmotif, which is enharmonically spelled F#-A-C#-E#, constitutes a link in the conversion of the original major third/major seventh chord D-F#-A-C# (Stefi's leitmotif) in the *Concerto*, into the minor third/major seventh chord F-Ab-C-E of the "funeral song" in the *First String Quartet* (1908–1909). Here we see at once that an autobiographical impression in the 1911 opera closes the procession of Bartók's autobiographical allusions in the works between 1907 and 1911. Ambling freely from one composition to another, the seventh chord appears to find its final destination on the operatic stage in the symbolic metamorphosis of the motif and Bartók's emotional turmoil. Thus the leitmotif that symbolizes Stefi Geyer carries a profound programmatic significance. From its melodic pattern and significance, and from the relationship itself, we begin to see counterparts between Stefi and Judith.

As we have shown at length, transformations from one form of the motif to another in the *Concerto* move through certain intervallic stages of compression and expansion. These stages are systematically outlined in the diagram above. For instance, the major seventh boundary on each four note-segment, combined with the succeeding transposition of the major seventh boundary, implies the presence of two half-steps that form the so-called x cell/ chromatic tetrachord. The transposition of the seventh chords by a progression of the fifth produces the chromatic tetrachords from the boundaries. And the ultimate disposition of the seventh chord progressions produces even and odd numbers of x cells. Furthermore, the root transpositions of these tetrachords outline respectively both whole tone scales. These symmetrical cyclic interval transformations stemming from the seventh chords are intermediary stages in the transformations and transpositions of the leitmotif. This ensures that the entire diagram is based on the principle of intervallic expansions and contractions, which are significant both for the symbolic meaning of the work and the integral connections of the pitch materials themselves. While the diagram is based on interlocking compounds of interval cycles, seventh chords, and the x motif (chromatic tetrachords) in both the *Violin Concerto* and *Bluebeard* opera, it records an element of the dramatic habitat in the story of both genres–bringing out the dissonant and painful element–in a process of contracting intervals from their tertian structure to the chromatic segments.

---

245 Indeed, both major and minor forms of Stefi's motif appear simultaneously at the occurrence of Judith's (i.e Stefi's) ideal *danger* motif.

Bartók himself refers to this as "chromatic compression.[246]" In *Bluebeard* the chromatic tetrachords signal transpositions of the blood motif,[247] and in the *Concerto*, Tristan's grief and desire (tunnel). And the seventh chords based on a varied tertian structure point to Judith's/Stefi's motif. Here the chromatic material has been transformed through its expansion–or as Bartók calls it, "extension in range"–into diatonic melodic motifs.[248]

Finally, let us take a brief look at the leitmotivic development of all these compositions in Bartók's early period. The leitmotivic structure in these works has its point of departure in his own identification of the motif (C#-E-G#-B#) that he mentions in his letter to Stefi in September 1907. It is the same but descending seventh chord construction (M3-M3-m3) that gives Judith her first entry: a descending melodic contour initiated on note F (F-Db-A-Gb) in *Bluebeard's Castle* (Rehearsal No. 3, m. 2). It is at this moment that Judith can be identified with Stefi as she now carries the leitmotif C#-E-G#-B# in the opera's setting for her own identity as part of her "danger" motif (no. 40). Antokoletz analyzes and interprets this as "part of the bimodal (major-minor third) clash, C#-E#-G#-B# versus C#-E-G#-B#," trembling and fearing the blood to come.[249] The C#-E-G#-B# outline (m3-M3-M3) as shown in the mid-September letter to Stefi, as well as its transposition to F-Ab-C-E in the initiating melody of the *First String Quartet*, is not the sound of the M3 that represents both love and joy. Rather, it is a m3 in a minor seventh chord (F-Ab-C-E) that represents sadness and melancholic superiority because happy times are now over. It is a motif that clearly speaks of Stefi's rejection. It is also this minor sounding motif of Stefi (C#-E-G#-B#) that is part of the dark sounding ostinato figures in *Bagatelle No. 13*, op. 6 (1908), "Elle est morte."

****

We have become witnesses to an idealistic fusion of two lives, and we have heard it sound in Bartók's music. We have argued that words can speak clearly about music, but music has its own grammar and vocabulary that only comes to full disclosure in the concert hall. And so we may still ask how poetic the nonverbal art can be. On the side of words, it is perhaps enough to speak about the romantic sphere the music reflects. Yet music can also color words and the worlds they

---

246 Antokoletz, *Musical Symbolism*, 24–25.
247 Antokoletz refers to this as to x-cell (G#-A-A3-B), a concentrated chromatic "blood" motif, which is presented in anticipation of Judith's first explicit reference to blood in the scene of the "Torture Chamber" (at nos. 30 and 34) in *Bluebeard's* opera, 199–200.
248 Antokoletz, *Musical Symbolism*, 24.
249 Ibid., 211.

image. For we can hear it when the music is there; we can feel it because we too have a heart, and we believe it because we have been witnesses to the life of the concerto and the concerto of two lives. Of course, it requires great sensitivity to distinguish such inflections. And to know the *Concerto* is to acknowledge its significance as a work of musical poetry in several aspects: a sophisticated and personal portrayal of two characters, an articulated and refined use of musical language, and a tightly-woven process and design. It was Bartók who projected singular thoughts and experiences into a creation of significant musical values; it is we who have the privilege to discover them.

In the wake of his unrequited relationship, Béla Bartók, as we know, became a brilliant creator of music and poetry–a human being who lived and composed, struggled and rejoiced, and narrated his knowledge, experience, and life in the profound language of his music. Stefi Geyer, the *Concerto* dedicatee, outlived the composer by eleven years. Lajos Nyikos informs us that "Stefi Geyer lived in Zurich and was known from 1926 on as Mrs. von Walter Schulthess."[250] After Stefi's death in 1956, in addition to the manuscript of the *1907 Violin Concerto*, "there were approximately thirty letters and other written documents" in her estate, which she had received from the 26-year-old Bartók as a young lady just 19 years old.[251] On May 30, 1958, the musical world in Basel welcomed the *Concerto's* premiere with soloist Hans-Heinz Schneeberger and conductor Paul Sacher.

But until its resurrection, Béla Bartók's *ideal* and *virtuoso* images of his beloved and the sounding out of his passions would lie dormant yet breathing in the silent *Concerto* for many years to come. The manuscript would find its fate sealed in a drawer of a locked desk until Stefi's death released it. Then it sprang to life: an electric love story waiting to be told and replayed by others–at once playful and plaintive, passing and permanent, like a sculpture that portrays some flesh and blood still laughing and crying through the marble. Those who do not know the story will still hear it told as through a manuscript darkly that shines some light each time the *Concerto* or its progeny is played. Those who do will hear an even more poignant song.

---

250 Béla Bartók, *Briefe an Stefi Geyer*, Introduction.
251 Ibid.

Appendix/Chronology

Béla Bartók's Letters to Stefi Geyer 1907–1908
Key to summaries

bold type	= direct quotes
italics	= paraphrase
(())	= musical quotation
BB	= Béla Bartók
SG	= Stefi Geyer

<u>No. 1, 2, 3,</u> etc., refer to the order of *Béla Bartók's Letters to Stefi Geyer* as seen in Lajos Nyikos' translation.

1907		
?		SG invites BB to Jászberény.
<u>No. 1</u>	(undated blue card)	BB announces his visit by SG on Friday at noon.
28 June		BB staying with SG & brother in Jászberény. *Concerto* quotes German folksong "Der Esel ist ein Dummes Tier" and this date is to be found in the second part/movement with mention of Jászberény and the date quoted.
01 July		BB begins work on *Concerto* in Jászberény.
?		BB attends SG performance with Bach *Chaconne*.
03 July		BB leaves for two-month folksong-collecting tour in Transylvania.
<u>No. 2</u>	from Rakospalota	BB to SG

		"On Sunday I was still comparing your hand with mine; however, on Tuesday I held a sun-burned hand of a peasant girl. On Sunday I spent the night in one of the most noble chamber-rooms, whereas on Tuesday, I got my rest in a peasant house."
?	(early July)	SG to BB (<u>letter</u> arrived in Csikrákos)
		"... a friendly voice, here on the wild desert!"
<u>No. 3</u>	from Csikrákos (14 July)	BB to SG
		"We only collect for a week and have already collected six such strange melodies that you can't find in Hungary." [5-tone scale/pentatonic or Székler's] Béla then chides Stefi for not having read any of the traditional classics such as Tolstoy or Nietzsche.
		"Everyone has read the 'Gartenlaube' literature by a certain age, if for no other reason than in the absence of better novels, or out of boredom. However, even we do not wish it, this reading has a small effect on us. You are missing the acquisition of knowledge; reading a few books can help. . . one more thing as far as the eternal fidelity subject. I'm not saying it's absolutely impossible; it's relative."
?	(mid July)	SG to BB (twelve-page <u>letter</u> arrived in Madaras)
<u>No. 4</u>	from Csikkarcfalva (27 July)	BB to SG (eight-page <u>letter</u>)

| | | "In Csíkrákos I was immediately told that a letter from "Stefi Geyer" had arrived for me in Madaras. Because of my work, however, I could not escape from this damned Csíkrákos, where I only had troubles! Torments of Tantalus! To know that your letter was so close by, just about 20 kilometers, and not to be able to get it! Yet even the worst of today will have something of a highpoint–in the future. In Madaras, after I had received your letter, I had to talk with strangers for a long time–I could not open your letter. But finally, even that happened. . . How can you only be so cruel to your own collector activity! How you ridicule and mock it! By the way, I am very impressed by the satirical tone you directed against yourself." |
| | | *[T]o be suspended between the highest stratum of society and mediocrity is an absolutely unbearable limitation. . . the lower level of society represents not mediocrity but the world of escape from urban civilization. It is the existence and actions of peasants that are most loved with their often pristine, childlike naivete. The upper level of society by way of contrast bespeaks a highly developed way of thought and emotional distance.* |

		((**Beethoven: C# minor S. Q. Op 131– 2nd movement main theme**)) *evokes a 'Grazioso' never more strongly felt.* **"I am very grateful to you for giving me a reason to offer these explanations, for they have left a mark on the question I was able to ask myself for the first time: what is the connection between the physical occurrence and, with that, the aroused feeling created by a chord like this one?"**
		((**Wagner: Tristan–opening grief motif**))
		. . .whereas this is weeping wretchedness.
		((**Strauss: Zarathustra–grave-song**))
No. 5	from Gyergyó-Kilyénfalva	BB to SG (<u>postcard</u>, 7. Aug)
?		SG to BB (<u>postcard</u> from Gyergyszentmiklos)
No. 6	from Gyergyó	BB to SG (The Folksong Collector in the villages of Karpaten)
?		SG to BB addressed to Szentdomokos, much-forwarded <u>letter</u> (re-quoted by BB in September 6th <u>letter</u>)
		"For life is beautiful! There is so much beauty in nature–the arts–science. . .I have no [religious] experience to speak of. . .I am no philosopher."
		SG feels 'sorry' for BB on account of his atheism. . . praises the Trinity. . . looks to the promised 'hereafter.'
		"I could fill a few more sheets with my scribbling, and I'd like to, but I can't. This evening I am going across to Buda."

No. 7	from Rákospalota (20 Aug)	BB to SG
		((**G. St. when she is smoking a pipe–2nd movement, main theme**)). . .*the portrait of the impetuous Stefi Geyer, humorous, witty and entertaining.*
No. 8	from Vésztő (6 Sept)	BB to SG (atheism)
		"Will you allow me to supply you with reading matter from time to time? (Something not too weighty as a start, just to bring you onto the right track; no middle-of-the-road stuff). You needn't be afraid that reading will blight your youth; even if it were to shorten it."
1 September		School year begins. Professor Bartók takes up admissions duties at Budapest Conservatory.
On Monday		BB meets with SG on September 9th.
		BB's "foolish, impatient departure" (mentioned in mid-September <u>letter</u>)
?		SG to BB (re-quoted by BB in September 11th <u>letter</u>)
		"There is not enough time or opportunity in the span of one life for us to win salvation." '*Serious music,' intellect and faith; distrusts BB's proposed reading list as a threat to her faith; condemns suicide as 'a cowardly act'; fears BB will attempt to talk her out of her faith; suggests they drop the subject; criticizes BB's recent impatient departure (Sept. 11th).*
No. 9	(Wednesday, Sept 11)	BB to SG (in reaction to SG's <u>letter</u>)

		With this letter begins the quarrel of religion between Béla and Stefi. Bartók's arguments are still quite mild, but in the following weeks, the fronts will harden.
		Atheism continues/Stefi's leitmotif
		"By the time I had finished reading your letter, I was almost in tears. . . After reading your letter, I sat down to the piano–I have a sad misgiving that I shall never find any consolation in life save in music. And yet–" ((Adagio molto, molto espr. [Inserted:] This is Your 'leitmotiv'))
On Thursday		BB meets SG (as announced in the above letter)
		"Not likely. . .arrive before 1 o'clock."
?		SG to BB
		Don't write unless it's about the 'Concerto.'
No. 10	from Rákospalota	BB to SG (16/17 at 2 a.m.)
		Bad, worse, much worse, the worst. . .The End. A nocturnal letter whose content shows a fivefold dramatic increase in word and deed.
		"Next time I'll come. . . I will try to pull out the serious word from you. (End)"
No. 11	Freitag (Sept. 20)	BB to SG
		"Your leitmotifs are buzzing all around me. All day long I live with you, in you, as in a narcotic dream."
		((Andante, quasi Adagio, und Allegro giocoso, und (Allegretto)))
		Stefi asks for forgiveness. . . Béla hopes for another visit; Sunday maybe too early, but Wednesday perhaps?

No. 12	(Sept. 26)	BB to SG (a postcard)
		((2nd movement, (toward the end)))
		"How would you score the accompaniment? Which is better?"
No. 13	(Oct. 14)	BB to SG (a postcard)
		"The purpose of my lines is to announce my visit tomorrow at half past two."
Nos. 14, 15, 16	(Oct. 27–28)	BB to SG (three postcards from: Nyitra, Daráž and Lapáš)
No. 17	(Nov. 26)	BB to SG (grey hour/motif)
		[W]hy did she receive him so warmly on their last two dates, even though his world had changed? His previous uncertainty regarding Stefi's feelings for him is now allayed. He has overcome his emotions. Music becomes his only consolation, and the strength of its language eclipses the paltry means of its verbal counterpart. . . [T]he chord appears to translate his mood into a sound, or perhaps to replace what he had attempted to verbalize. Its last appearance comes during
		"the 'grey hour': just before the day broke–I should not have written–what is the use to rub the. . . 'motif-image' in such manner!"
		The 'grey reality' is what is left and BB will be a slave to it–this is the world he knew–moors competing with wasteland, indifference mirrored in dullness. He will adore this world until death liberates him. He had no one from the start that his friendship with Stefi was a challenge and maybe hopeless, yet he instinctively looked for the next step.

?		SG to BB (a <u>postcard</u> from Leipzig; re-quoted in the next BB <u>letter</u>)
		"However, it was not so much the external thing that made me so happy, it was the fact that you were thinking about me while being so far away."
<u>No. 18</u>	(Nov. 29)	BB to SG
		((Stefi's motif))
		". . .for this is where I did not betray myself."
		"Especially during these hours I thought a lot about you, the main theme of the second movement in your *Concerto* was born: also from the latter this and that are derived. Although it is "better" for me that you are not here, I wished so much for you to be here. Could you tell me when you will come home, how many days before Christmas Eve, and then how long you will stay? I would like to harmonize it–in consonances!–just this once on your behalf–these data with my collection-trips."
		((2nd movement theme))
		"But you are rather close to that picture. . .Composing the second movement I will succeed I think! However, I wish it would be reversed. . . Though one does not have to be always 6/8 D-F$^\sharp$-A-C$^\sharp$, one has to be some-time. . . ((2nd movement theme)). . . No, ((Stefi's motif)) cannot be redeemed from me–even I have tried."

		Ideal portrait of Stefi's 'Jászberény reality,' other portrait, one of coolness and speechless with anger yet to be written.
		"But it will be an awful music."
		((Stefi-motif and Tristan chord))
		Bartók visits with Stefi's mother on the afternoon of Nov. 30th.
<u>No. 19</u>	(Saturday, Nov. 30)	BB to SG
		Bartók sends his regards and hearty congratulations after seeing the wonderful critics following Stefi's recent solo performance and its enormous success.
<u>No. 20</u>	(Dec. 8)	BB to SG
		"Only this tangled thought hammers as an 'idée fixe' in my head: nowhere, neither in art nor in friendship, is there any success–only failure. . . No, I cannot separate myself from ((Stefi's ideal image)), even I have tried."
		Bartók wants to know, therefore, asks Stefi what she is thinking and feeling while listening to something that in reality is of no interest to her.
		"Do you know what the piece means for me? No, you do not know; so I will answer: everything. And for you?"
?		SG to BB (<u>letter</u>/mid-December)
		"[I]t occurred to me, that I shouldn't go–perhaps later some day–until then do as you please."
<u>No. 21</u>	(Dec. 21)	BB to SG (planning a meeting on Saturday or Sunday)
		"How much did I await this letter."

		"It is not 'crossheit' [anger] that is expressed in it: it is 'female' cruelty. . . How can one survive such torment? And you yourself remind me to take care of my health."
		((2nd movement theme))
		'Concerto' must be in 2 movements only–2 opposites of one portrait. Bartók wonders why did true recognition come to him so late?
		"This is the reality of Jászberény, that is an 'ideal image.' A man opens his eyes rather seldom."
No. 22	(Dec. 23)	BB to SG (First draft of *Concerto's* manuscript is finished as a Christmas gift for its dedicatee–his "death warrant.")
		From 9:00 p.m. in the evening until 6:00 a.m. on the morning of December 24th, Bartók works uninterruptedly to finish the 'Concerto,' partly taking it out of sketches with some parts still in pencil to have it ready for Stefi to look at on Christmas.
1908		
No. 23	(Jan. 7, 9, and 14)	BB's diary entries
		["G]aze of her eyes will be my only consolation, my sanctuary, my all and everything during the long solitude of her absence. . . All is in vain, even my last hope I shall have to renounce!"
		Based on their last encounters, it had become obvious to Bartók that there was not even one sliver of hope that might give him any cause for consolation.
?		SG to BB

		((See you in February. Until then all the best))
No. 24	(30 Jan.)	BB to SG (from Vienna)
		((glowing theme))
		"I could have indeed even rejoiced that you had made this glowing theme your own. Not even to mention that perhaps you could understand it differently from the way I do. Now I see in it only straw, like leftover straw that you have handed me in my agony of death."
		Bartók repeats often. . . .it cannot go on like this.
?		SG to BB (Dortmund letter)
No. 25	(8 Feb.)	BB to SG (last dated letter)
		On February 8th, 1908 Béla Bartók declares his farewell and takes his leave forever:
		"I have begun a quartet: the first theme is the theme of the Concerto's 2nd movement; this is my funeral dirge."
		"So, I must take my leave (farewell) for ever now, because this is the last time that I am writing! The last time! So, on that Saturday then I played with you for the last time, and on Monday evening, I spoke my last words to you by a barrier of the underground subway. For the last time I listened to you, for the last time I saw you. For the last time! Don't these words fit to one, who prepares for his death, only?"
5 February		The last version of the *Concerto* is finished!

13 February		SG to BB
		It's over.
14 February		BB composes *Bagatelle No. 13*, inscribing "Elle est morte" over Stefi's motif.
?		BB to SG
		"Now it's going to be a year (since we have gotten to know each other). How often have I thought of this sad, imminent anniversary–because I cannot forget you, for I still love you the same as before. And you therefore think of me too because you still love me. These eight to ten words on Thursday–they said it with full trepidation–your expression in the evening–no indifferent human soul looks like that; in such circumstances no indifferent feeling speaks like that."
		"I am already happy if I only know that you love me and that I can see you. Otherwise I don't need anything... I love you so and as such as you are."
		He loves her the way she is, the way he has known her from the start, and absolutely in no other way.
16 February		BB sends the *Concerto* to SG with a poem by Béla Balázs as postscript...and he does it because he believes that she still loves him.

List of Works Consulted

Abbate, Carolyn. *Unsung Voices: Opera and Musical Narrative in the Nineteenth Century*. Princeton, NJ: Princeton University Press, 1991.

Antokoletz, Elliott. "Principles of Pitch Organization in Bartók's *Fourth String Quartet*." New York, NY: Ph.D. diss. City University of New York, 1975.

_____. *The Music of Béla Bartók*. Berkeley and Los Angeles, CA: University of California Press, 1984.

_____. "Bartók's Bluebeard: The Sources of Its Modernism." *College Music Symposium 30/1* (Spring 1990), 75–95.

_____. *Béla Bartók: A Guide to Research, Second Edition*. New York and London: Garland Publishing, Inc., 1997.

_____. *Bartók Perspectives*. Edited by Elliott Antokoletz, Victoria Fischer, and Benjamin Suchoff. New York and Oxford: Oxford University Press, 2000.

_____. *Musical Symbolism in the Operas of Debussy and Bartók*. New York and Oxford: Oxford University Press, 2004.

Apthorp, William F. "Some of Wagner's Heroes and Heroines." *Scribner's Magazine 5* (1889), 331–348.

Bartók, Béla. *Béla Bartók Essays*. Edited by Benjamin Suchoff. New York, NY: St. Martin's Press, 1976.

_____. *Béla Bartók Essays*. Selected and Edited by Benjamin Suchoff. Lincoln, NE and London: University of Nebraska Press, 1992.

_____. *Briefe an Stefi Geyer*. Edited by Paul Sacher. German Translation by Lajos Nyikos. Basel: Privatdruck Ltd., 1979.

Batta, András. "Gemeinsames Nietzsche-Symbol bei Bartók und bei R. Strauss." *Studia Musicologica 24/3–4* (1982), 275–282.

Botstein, Leon. "Out of Hungary: Bartók, Modernism, and the Cultural Politics of Twentieth-Century Music." *Bartók and His World*. Edited by Peter Laki. Princeton, NJ: Princeton University Press, 1995, 49.

Bónis, Ferenc. "Bartók und Wagner. Paul Sacher zum 75. Geburtstag." *Österreichische Musikzeitschrift 36* (1981), 134–147.

_____. *Béla Bartók: His Life in Pictures and Documents*. Budapest: Corvina Press, 1981.

_____. "Erstes Violinkonzert–Erstes Streichquartett: Ein Wendepunkt in Béla Bartók's kompositorischer Laufbahn." *Musica 39/3* (1985), 265–273.

Buckley, Michael J. *At the Origins of Modern Atheism*. New Haven: Yale University Press, 1987, 145–250.

Chalmers, Kenneth. "Portrait of a Girl 1907–9." *Béla Bartók*. London: Phaidon Press, 1995, 56–80.

Collins, James. *God in Modern Philosophy*. Chicago: Henry Regnery, 1959.

Crawford, Dorothy L. "Love and Anguish." *Bartók Perspectives*. Edited by Elliott Antokoletz, Victoria Fischer, and Benjamin Suchoff. New York and Oxford: Oxford University Press, 2000, 129–139.

Crow, Todd. *Bartók Studies*. Detroit: Information Coordinators, 1976.

Dahlhaus, Carl. *Between Romanticism and Modernism*. Translated by Mary Whittall. Berkeley and Los Angeles, CA: University of California Press, 1980.

_____. *Nineteenth-Century Music*. Translated by James Bradford Robinson. Berkeley and Los Angeles, CA: University of California Press, 1989.

Demény, János. *Béla Bartók Letters*. Budapest: Corvina Press, 1971. Edited by Peter Balabán and István Farkas. Translation revised by Elisabeth West and Colin Mason. New York: St. Martin's Press, 1971.

Dille, Denijs. "Angaben zum Violinkonzert 1907, den Deux Portraits, dem Quartett op.7 und den Zwei Rumänischen Tänzen." *Documenta Bartókiana, vol. 2*. Edited Denijs Dille. Mainz: Schott, 1965, 91–103.

_____. "Bartók, Reader of Nietzsche and of La Rochefoucauld." *Studia Musicologica 10* (1968), 209–228.

Fischer, Victoria. "Bartók's Fourteen Bagatelles op. 6, for Piano: Toward Performance Authenticity," *Bartók Perspectives*. Edited by Elliott Antokoletz, Victoria Fisher, and Benjamin Suchoff. New York and Oxford: Oxford University Press, 2000, 273–286.

Frigyesi, Judit. *Béla Bartók and Turn-of-the-Century Budapest*. Berkeley and Los Angeles, CA: University of California Press, 1998.

Gillies, Malcolm. *Bartók Remembered*. New York and London: Norton, 1991.

_____. "Stylistic Integrity and Influence on Bartók's Works: The Case of Szymanowski." *International Journal of Musicology vol. 1* (1992), 139–160.

_____. "Portraits, Pictures and Pieces." *The Bartók Companion*. Edited by Malcolm Gillies. London: Faber and Faber, 1993.

_____. "Two Orchestral Suites." *The Bartók Companion*. Edited by Malcolm Gillies. London: Faber and Faber, 1993, 454–466.

Gow, David. "Tonality and Structure in Bartók's First Two String Quartets." *The Music Review 34* (August–November 1973), 459–471.

Hoffman, Ernst Theodor A. "Beethoven's Instrumental Music." *Source Readings in Music History*. Edited by Oliver Strunk. New York: Norton, 1950, 775–781.

Kárpáti, János. *Bartók's String Quartets*. Translated by Fred Macnicol. Budapest: Corvina Press, 1975; original Hungarian edition, Budapest: Zeneműkiadó, 1967, 173.

————. "Early String Quartets." *The Bartók Companion*. Edited by Malcolm Gillies. London: Faber and Faber, 1993, 226–242.

Kramer, Lawrence. *Music as Cultural Practice 1800–1900*. Berkeley and Los Angeles, CA: University of California Press, 1990.

Levarie, Siegmund. "Musical Polarity: Major and Minor." *International Journal of Musicology 1* (1992), 29–45.

Magee, Bryan. *Aspects of Wagner*. Oxford and New York: Oxford University Press, 1988.

Marston, Nicholas. *Schumann: Fantasie, Op. 17*. Cambridge: Cambridge University Press, 1992.

Nattiez, Jean-Jaques. "Can One Speak of Narrativity in Music?" *Journal of the Nineteenth Century Princeton 115/2* (1991), 242–257.

Newcomb, Anthony. "Once more 'Between Absolute and Program Music:' Schumann's Second Symphony." *Nineteenth-Century Music VII/3* (1984), 233–249.

————. "Schumann and Late Eighteenth-Century Narrative Strategies". *Nineteenth-Century Music XI/2* (1987), 164–174.

Petho, Berthalan. "The Meaning of Bartók's Secret Path." *Studia Musicologica 24* (1982), 405–413.

Somfai, László. "A Characteristic Culmination Point in Bartók's Instrumental Forms." *International Musicologica Conference in Commemoration of Béla Bartók*, 1971. Edited by József Ujfalussy and János Breuer. New York, NY: Belwin Mills, 1972, 53–64.

Stevens, Halsey. *The Life and Music of Béla Bartók*. New York: Oxford University Press, 1953.

Suchoff, Benjamin. *The Hungarian Folk Song*. Translated by Michel-Dimitri Calvocoressi. Albany, NY: State University of New York, 1981.

————. *Concerto for Orchestra: Understanding Bartók's World*. New York: Schirmer Books, 1995.

Szabolcsi, Bence. *Béla Bartók, Weg und Werk, Schriften und Briefe*. Edited by Bence Szabolcsi. Budapest: Corvina Press, 1957.

Treitler, Leo. "Harmonic Procedure in the Fourth String Quartet of Béla Bartók." *Journal of Music Theory 3/2* (1959), 292–297.

Ujfalussy, József. *Bartók Béla*. English Translation by Ruth Pataki. Translation revised by Elisabeth West. Budapest: Corvina Press, 1971.

Vikárius, László. *Modell és Inspiráció: Bartók zenei gondolkodásában*. Pécs: Jelenkor Kiadó, 1999.

Weiss-Aigner, Günter. "The Lost Violin Concerto." *The Bartók Companion*. Edited by Malcolm Gillies. London: Faber and Faber, 1993, 468–476.

Zielinski, Tadeusz A. *Bartók*. Kraków: Wydawnictwo Muzyczne, 1969.

QUELLEN UND STUDIEN ZUR MUSIKGESCHICHTE VON DER ANTIKE BIS IN DIE GEGENWART
SOURCES AND STUDIES IN MUSIC HISTORY FROM ANTIQUITY TO THE PRESENT

Herausgegeben von / Edited by Elliott Antokoletz, Michael von Albrecht

Band   1 Musik in Antike und Neuzeit. Unter Mitwirkung zahlreicher Fachgelehrter herausgegeben von Michael von Albrecht und Werner Schubert. 1987.

Band   2 Georg von Albrecht: Gesamtausgabe, Band 1: Sämtliche Klavierwerke, nach den Handschriften erstmals vollständig herausgegeben von Michael von Albrecht. 1984.

Band   3 Georg von Albrecht: Vom Volkslied zur Zwölftontechnik. Schriften und Erinnerungen eines Musikers zwischen Ost und West, herausgegeben von Michael von Albrecht. 1984.

Band   4 Michael von Albrecht: Goethe und das Volkslied. 2. Auflage, mit einer Bibliographie von Werner Schubert. 1985.

Band   5 Hermann Schäfer: Lieder und Gesänge für eine Singstimme und Klavier. 1985.

Band   6 Georg von Albrecht: Gesamtausgabe, Band 2: Lieder, nach den Handschriften erstmals vollständig herausgegeben von Michael von Albrecht. 1986.

Band   7 Wenzel Hübner: 21000 Orgeln aus aller Welt 1945-1985. 1986.

Band   8 Georg von Albrecht: Gesamtausgabe, Band 6: Streichquartette und Streichtrio, mit einem Facsimile von op. 52. Nach den Handschriften erstmals herausgegeben von Michael von Albrecht. 1986.

Band   9 Wilfried Neumaier: Was ist ein Tonsystem? Eine historisch-systematische Theorie der abendländischen Tonsysteme, gegründet auf die antiken Theoretiker Aristoxenos, Eukleides und Ptolemaios, dargestellt mit Mitteln der modernen Algebra. 1986.

Band 10 Georg von Albrecht: Gesamtausgabe, Band 3: Chorwerke und größere Vokalwerke mit einem Facsimile des 'Liedes der Lieder'. Nach den Handschriften herausgegeben von Werner Schubert. 1988.

Band 11 Georg von Albrecht: Gesamtausgabe, Band 4: Kammermusik für Streicher und Klavier: Werke für Violine und Klavier, Violoncello und Klavier, Viola und Klavier, Klaviertrio. Nach den Handschriften herausgegeben von Christiane von Albrecht. 1987.

Band 12 Georg von Albrecht: Gesamtausgabe, Band 5: Solostücke für Violine, Violin-Duette, Solostücke für Violoncello. Nach den Handschriften erstmals herausgegeben von Michael von Albrecht. 1987.

Band 13 Gerhard Frommel: Tradition und Originalität. Schriften und Vorträge zur Musik. Unter Mitwirkung von Wolfgang Osthoff herausgegeben von Michael von Albrecht. 1987.

Band 14 Georg von Albrecht: Gesamtausgabe, Band 7: Orchesterwerke, herausgegeben von Michael von Albrecht. 1991.

Band 15 Georg von Albrecht: Gesamtausgabe, Band 8: Bühnenwerke, erstmals herausgegeben von Michael von Albrecht. 1991.

Band 16 Georg von Albrecht: Gesamtausgabe, Band 9: Orgelwerke, nach den Handschriften erstmals herausgegeben von Wolfgang Dallmann. 1987.

Band 17 Egert Pöhlmann: Beiträge zur antiken und neueren Musikgeschichte. 1988.

Band 18 Rudolf Walter: Johann Caspar Ferdinand Fischer, Hofkapellmeister der Markgrafen von Baden. 1990.

Band 19 Jean-Bernard Condat (Ed.): Nombre d'Or et Musique. Goldener Schnitt und Musik. Golden Section and Music. 1988.

Band 43 Elliott Antokoletz: The Musical Language of the Twentieth Century. The Discovery of a Missing Link. The Music of Georg von Albrecht. 2012.

Band 44 Hans-Peter Retzmann: Max Regers Musik. Eine Studie zu Regers Musikdenken. 2015.

Band 45 Antje Reineke: Benjamin Brittens Liederzyklen. 2015.

Band 46 John K. Novak: The Symphonic Works of Leoš Janáček. From Folk Concepts to Original Style. 2016.

Band 47 Johnny Reinhard: Bach and Tuning. 2016.

Band 48 Monica Kang: Post-Tonal Affinities in Piano Works of Bartók, Chen, and Crumb. 2016.

Band 49 Aloyse Michaely: Das verwehrte Opfer. Strawinskys biblisches Alterswerk *Abraham and Isaac* mit einem Blick zurück auf *The Flood*. 2017.

Band 50 Alicja Usarek-Topper: Béla Bartók's *1907 Violin Concerto*: Genesis and Fate. 2020.

www.peterlang.com